George M. Towle

Heroes and Martyrs of Invention

George M. Towle

Heroes and Martyrs of Invention

ISBN/EAN: 9783337194246

Printed in Europe, USA, Canada, Australia, Japan

Cover: Foto ©Andreas Hilbeck / pixelio.de

More available books at **www.hansebooks.com**

HEROES AND MARTYRS

OF

INVENTION

BY

GEORGE MAKEPEACE TOWLE

AUTHOR OF "VASCO DA GAMA: HIS VOYAGES AND ADVENTURES" "PIZARRO: HIS
ADVENTURES AND CONQUESTS" "MAGELLAN; OR, THE FIRST VOYAGE ROUND
THE WORLD" "MARCO POLO: HIS TRAVELS AND ADVENTURES" "RALEIGH:
HIS VOYAGES AND ADVENTURES" "DRAKE, THE SEA KING OF DEVON"
"YOUNG PEOPLE'S HISTORY OF ENGLAND" "YOUNG PEOPLE'S
HISTORY OF IRELAND" "THE NATION IN A NUTSHELL"

BOSTON MDCCCXC
LEE AND SHEPARD PUBLISHERS
10 MILK STREET NEXT "THE OLD SOUTH MEETING HOUSE"
NEW YORK CHAS. T. DILLINGHAM
718 AND 720 BROADWAY

CONTENTS

HEROES AND MARTYRS OF INVENTION

CHAPTER I

EARLY INVENTORS

A N IMPOSING CEREMONY took place not
long ago in the ancient historic city of
Syracuse, in the Island of Sicily. A tardy
statue was raised by the Syracusans to their
most famous man, who has been two thousand years in his grave.

The statue looks out upon the purple waters
of the beautiful bay, which, nearly two centuries before Christ, witnessed some of those
signal triumphs of science, which have ren-
dered the name of Archimedes forever illustrious.

In the authentic history of invention, indeed, the name of Archimedes stands earliest

and first. No doubt there were many inventors, and great inventors, before his time ; but
Archimedes is the first known inventor whose
astonishing labors have come down to us in
clear and trustworthy narrative. He is, therefore, entitled to be called the patriarch of
science.

And the more we learn of this wonderful
Syracusan, the more we marvel at the ingenuity of his genius, and the creative power
of his intellect. He is declared to have been
equally skilled in all the sciences ; in astronomy and geometry, in hydrostatics, dynam-
ics, and optics. He was the parent of the
art of civil engineering. He was the author
of a great number of precious inventions. He
established the modern system of measuring
curved surfaces and solids.

He was the first to prove the important fact
"that a body plunged into a fluid loses as
much of its weight as is equal to the weight
of an equal volume of the fluid." The way

in which he discovered this principle is curious and interesting.

His cousin, Hiero, King of Syracuse, wishing to make an offering to the gods of a golden crown, ordered a certain goldsmith to make one for him. It was soon found, however, that the goldsmith had dishonestly made part of the crown of silver. Hiero called upon Archimedes to find out how much silver had been inserted in the crown.

The philosopher was perplexed; but one day, while taking a brimming bath, Archimedes observed that the quantity of water which overflowed was just equal to the bulk of his own body. Leaping out of the bath, he ran homeward, exultantly crying: "Eureka! I have found it!"

He now made two masses, one of gold and one of silver. Filling a vessel brim full of water, he alternately inserted in it the gold and the silver mass. He thus found the measures of water which answered to a cer-

tain quantity of each of the two metals;
thereby proved the comparative weight of
gold and of silver; and was able to show just
how much of the baser metal had been inserted in the golden crown.

The whole life of Archimedes was romantic.
His scientific triumphs were striking and brilliant, and the influence of his absorbing labors
was marked and enduring upon the progress
of the human race.   His most noted achievement, perhaps, was the part he took in de-
fending his native Syracuse from the assault
of the Romans under Marcellus.

The city was sore besieged by the Roman
galleys.   It seemed as if nothing could avert
its doom.

"The vigorous attempts made by Marcellus
to carry Syracuse by storm," says Livy, the
Roman historian, "had certainly sooner succeeded but for the interposition of one man,
Archimedes; famous for his skill in astronomy, but still more so for his surprising in-

vention of warlike machines. By these, in an instant, he destroyed what had cost his enemy vast labor to construct. Against the Roman vessels, which came up close to the city, he contrived a kind of crow or crane, projected above the battlements, with an iron grapple attached to a strong chain. This was let down on the prow of a ship, and, by means of the weight of a heavy counterpoise of lead, it raised up the prow, and set the vessel upright on her end."

Another story, the truth of which was long doubted by philosophers, but the probability of which has been shown by the later discoveries of science, is, that Archimedes set the Roman ships on fire by means of mirrors. When the ships were within bow-shot of the shore, Archimedes placed some hexagonal and smaller mirrors, each at a proper distance, opposite the sun, and moved them by means of hinges and metal plates. Directed upon the ships, these were set on fire, and were burned as if by the operation of magic.

The possibility of this remarkable feat of science has since been many times shown. It is asserted that in the sixth century a famous man of science, Proclus, set fire to the Thracian fleet in the harbor of Constantinople, by means of mirrors made of brass. In the last century, the great French naturalist, Buffon, repeated with success the exploit attributed to Archimedes at Syracuse. Buffon, with his apparatus of mirrors, set fire to planks at a distance of two hundred feet, and melted metals and minerals at a distance of forty feet.

In our own day, the problem how to use the heat of the sun by mechanical agency is one of the most absorbing objects of the search of natural philosophers. One of these has recently been bold enough to assert that on any space in the United States, twenty by thirty miles square, enough of the heat of the sun is wasted to drive all the steam engines in the world.

In spite of the well-nigh superhuman efforts of Archimedes in behalf of the proud and lovely city of his birth, it was at length carried by surprise by the Roman legions. As the exultant victors swarmed through the streets, they found Archimedes quietly seated in the public square.

His head was bent, and he was deeply studying a series of geometrical figures, which he had just traced in the sand. He did not seem to be conscious that the city had been captured, or that the Romans had invaded its streets. A Roman soldier, not knowing who he was, ran up to the absorbed philosopher with a drawn sword. Archimedes perceived his murderous intent.

" Hold your hand a little," said he quietly, glancing at the figures in the sand ; " only spare my life until I have solved this problem."

But the petition fell on heedless ears ;

and this greatest man of his age perished by the hand of the rude barbarian. Archimedes was buried with imposing funeral pomp.

Upon his tombstone, in accordance with his own desire, was engraved a cylinder bearing a sphere; a device which represented his discovery of the proportion between a cylinder and a sphere of the same diameter.

But in the hurly-burly of the time he was soon, and for long, forgotten. A hundred and fifty years later, Cicero, wandering in Syracuse, found the tombstone, neglected, lost sight of, and overgrown with weeds and thistles.

And now, at last, in the nineteenth century, Syracuse has remembered her illustrious ancient citizen, and has fittingly reared a *statue* to his memory.

In his great lecture on "The Lost Arts," Wendell Phillips described many inventions the knowledge of which had become extinct, though the products of those lost inventions

still survive. He told of others which, having become extinct, had been again revived
in later ages.

The re-discovery of ancient and once lost
arts, indeed, is a striking phase of the history
of mediæval and modern invention. Many of
the most signal scientific triumphs of later
times were known at periods concerning which
only dim traditions remain.

Some of the uses of steam were known to
the ancients, who employed it to grind drugs,
to turn spits, and to amuse and to terrify the
common people. It is stated by antiquaries
that the Romans knew the art of printing;
but opposed the practice of it, because it
deprived the scribes of their avocation.
Certain it is that the Romans made imprints
upon their pottery by means of stereotypes.

Printing was known to the Chinese in
remote antiquity ; and lithography had been
a familiar German art three centuries before
its re-discovery less than a hundred years ago.

The Romans quite understood the properties of gunpowder; but rather played and trifled with it, as they did with steam, than put it to any useful service. As they made steam a bugbear, so they used gunpowder mainly for fireworks.

It is certain that Colt's revolver is only a re-discovery of an ancient weapon; for in the Arsenal of Venice you may see not only revolvers, but rifled muskets and breech-loading cannon, which were made and used in the fifteenth century.

Locomotion by steam was attempted by Blasco da Garay, in the harbor of Barcelona, two centuries and a half before Robert Fulton guided the famous "Clermont" up the Hudson. Dr. Darwin predicted the locomotive and the steamboat, a quarter of a century before Fulton's memorable trip, in the oft-quoted lines, —

"Soon shall thy arm, unconquered steam! afar
Drag the slow barge, and drive the rapid car!"

When the tunnel was built beneath the Thames, it was believed to be indeed a new thing under the sun; a marvel of modern engineering skill. But it was afterwards found that tunnels had been laid beneath the waters of the Euphrates at ancient Babylon. The Romans built excellent macadamized roads. The idea of the Congreve rocket was borrowed by its re-inventor from the ingenious arsenals of Hindostan. The Chinese, ages ago, lit their houses with coal-gas.

If there is any modern discovery to which we should be most strongly tempted to attribute absolute originality, it would be that of the anæsthetic properties and uses of ether. But in the works of Albertus Magnus, who lived in the thirteenth century, — in the midst of the hurly-burly of the Crusades, — you will find a good practical recipe for preparing ether as an anæsthetic. The same principle, indeed, was known to many ancient peoples. In the far East, nepenthe and mandragora were used to deaden pain. To a similar purpose the Chinese put mayo, and the Egyptians their soothing and seductive hasheesh.

It was supposed that glass was a discovery of mediæval times, until specimens of it were found in the more elegant of the lava-buried villas of Pompeii.

We must abandon, too, the proud and cherished belief that the electric telegraph was the original device of an illustrious American of the nineteenth century. "The invention of the telegraph," says a recent English scientific writer, "was clearly indicated by Schwenter in 1636. He then pointed out how two persons could communicate with each other by means of the magnetic needle." A century later, in 1746, Le Mounier exhibited a series of experiments in the Royal Gardens at Paris, showing how electricity could be transmitted through iron wire nine hundred fathoms in length.

But a real electric telegraph was actually set to work, in 1774, by Le Sage of Geneva. His instrument comprised twenty-four metallic wires, separated and enclosed in a nonconducting substance. Each wire ended in a stalk, mounted with a little ball of elderwood, suspended by a silk thread. A slight stream of electricity was sent through the wire; the elder ball at the other end was repelled; and this repulsion indicated a letter of the alphabet.

A device very much like that of Le Sage was invented a few years later by Lomond of Paris.

The discovery that the sun can paint pictures on a plate prepared with certain chemicals, can by no means be justly claimed by Monsieur Daguerre, although he gave his name to the daguerreotype. To the renowned artist who, four centuries ago, decorated the walls of the stately Refectory at Milan with his splendid picture of "The Last Supper," who contended with Michael Angelo for the artistic sceptre of Florence, and who was not only a painter and sculptor of the highest genius, but was also a noted chemist, a successful engineer, a melodious poet, a graceful musician, and an ardent astronomer; to Leonardo da Vinci the world perhaps owes the great idea of photography, which has given so much aid to science, and so much pleasure, instruction, and delight to all mankind.

Six hundred years ago, old Friar Bacon taught his countrymen that many of the wonders which, in their ignorance, they attributed to sorcery, to the machinations of the Evil One, to the weird agency of ghosts and witches, were really works of nature, or of skilful human art.

It is almost startling, indeed, to see how this learned and far-seeing English monk, of an almost barbaric period, imagined and clearly foreshadowed some of the greatest inventions of modern times. " Instruments may be made," he says, " by which the largest ships, with only one man guiding them, will be carried with greater swiftness than if they were full of sailors. Chariots may be built that will move with incredible rapidity, without the help of animals. Instruments of flying may be formed, in which a man, sitting at his ease, may beat the air with his artificial wings, after the manner of birds. A small instrument may be made to raise and depress the greatest weights. An instrument may be devised by which a man may draw a thousand men to him by force, and against their will. Machines can be constructed which will enable men to walk at the bottom of seas or rivers without danger."

. So it was that this bright morning star, rising in the dim dawn of modern science, shot its penetrating ray far athwart the shadows of the future ; and discerned, almost clearly, locomotion by steam, the perfection of the principle of the lever, the sounding of the mysterious ocean depths by the diving-bell, and the successful navigation of the air.

CHAPTER II

LAURENCE COSTER, THE DISCOVERER OF TYPE-PRINTING

In Holland there is a very ancient town called Haarlem. It is a drowsy, humdrum old place, with quaint houses of many gables, and irregular grass-grown streets, and long reaches of straight, stagnant canals. Some of the streets are so narrow that you can shake hands with a passer-by on the opposite sidewalk, and in some places the upper stories project so far over the lower ones that two people in opposite houses can easily converse with each other.

On one of these streets stands a house which seems even older than most of its neighbors. It looks as if it were toppling over, and might fall down over the rough sidewalk any windy day. Its windows are full of tiny, dust-covered panes, and its single upper story so projects as to form a shelter and shade over the doorway. This old house is pointed out to strangers who go to Haarlem to see the curiosities of the venerable town as one of especial interest. It is said to be at least six or seven centuries old. But the reason why it is especially worth seeing is that once upon a time, long, long ago, there dwelt in it a man of whom the sedate people of Haarlem are still very proud. His name was Laurence Coster. He was the warden of a little church which stood not far from his modest dwelling, and passed his time between his not very heavy duties at the church and in the midst of his family at home.

Among other tastes, Laurence Coster was very fond of reading. He lived, indeed, five hundred years ago ; and at that period, it need not be said, there were no printed books such as we have now. The only books which then existed were those written on parchment and vellum, and this was done mainly by the monks in their quiet monasteries. It followed that these written books were very rare and expensive. They were not to be found in the homes of the people. Even a great and rich lord could only afford to have a very few of them. They were as much of a luxury in a rich household as a picture by a famous artist is now.

Of course, as books were so scarce and expensive, very few of the common people ever learned how to read. But Laurence Coster was an exception to this rule. He had always been a great student, fond of learning, and preferring solitude to the society of those around him. In the little church of which he was warden there were a few of the monks' manuscript volumes ; and these, we may well believe, Coster had read over and over until he must have well-nigh known them by heart.

Thus Coster lived on to middle age, and

then to old age, in a quiet, humdrum, studious existence. He now found his little home peopled with quite a family. His son had married, and lived with him in the old house, and three or four rosy grandchildren delighted Coster's declining years. To give pleasure to these grandchildren, and to teach them what he himself knew, became the joy of his old age.

Old Coster was very fond of strolling by himself in the outskirts of the quiet town. Sometimes, attired in his short seedy cloak, and a hat which was shaped like a sugar-loaf, and had a broad flapping brim, he would saunter along the banks of the slow little river Spaaren, which wound beyond the town. But his favorite haunt was a dense grove which stood a mile or two beyond the limits of Haarlem, and which was little resorted to by any one except himself.

This grove had for many a year been a retreat to which Coster had loved to resort.

When he had been a young man, full of senti-
ment and romantic notions, he had gone out
to it to dream of the fair maid of his love.
Even now, in old age, he could find on one of
the trees the letters which formed the initials
of her name, which he had once fondly carved
there when in a sentimental mood.

In a different way this habit of carving
letters in the bark of the trees still seemed to
delight him. When of a languid summer
afternoon he stretched himself out on the
short soft moss beneath a beech-tree, he would
almost unconsciously tear off some of the
bark and begin to fashion letters from it with
his knife. One day it occurred to him not
only to carve the letters, but to cut them out,
put them in his pocket, and carry them home.
He thought that it would be the easiest possible way to teach his little grandchildren their
alphabet, and so in time enable them to read,
if he showed them the letters in the form of
playthings.

After a while this became a regular custom with him. He was delighted to see that the letters of bark greatly amused the children, and that they very soon learned to tell one from another. Then the old man became more careful and more skilful in carving the letters. He tried to fashion them as nicely and distinctly as possible, and spent more hours than ever in the grove, absorbed in this pleasant occupation, which was destined to make him famous.

One afternoon Coster had been more than usually successful in cutting the letters out of the bark. His old eyes twinkled to see how neatly he had made them. He happened to have an old piece of parchment with him, and with this he carefully wrapped up the letters and carried them home in his pocket.

The grandchildren, as usual, were watching eagerly for their dearly loved old grandsire, and as he approached, ran out to meet him and lead him by both hands into the house.

They clapped their hands with glee when he took the piece of parchment from his pocket, and, unfolding it, showed them a number of prettier letters than they had ever seen before. They at once took the letters, and vied with each other in pronouncing them, while the old man playfully corrected their mistakes. Meanwhile the old scrap of parchment had been thrown carelessly aside. But it happened that one of the little boys, tired for the moment of playing with the letters, picked up the parchment and unfolded it. Then he cried out in wonder, " Look, grandfather ! see what the letters have done ! "

Coster took the parchment from the boy to see what he meant. His eyes dilated as he gazed upon the parchment. There, upon its surface, the letters had left a clear imprint. To be sure, the imprint represented the letters reversed, but nevertheless they were there, printed upon the parchment. It soon appeared that when Coster had carved the letters the bark had been moist with the sap of the tree, and the sap had performed the service of ink.

Old Coster, though a man in a humble sphere of life, was very far from being a dull one. His thoughtful, studious life enabled him to perceive that this printing of the bark letters on the parchment was really a great discovery. What if, by thus having a series of letters, and impressing them again and again upon parchment, books might be multiplied and made cheap for all the world!

Laurence Coster now had a new occupation in life, which absorbed all his hours and labors. By a mere accident, as it seemed, he had discovered the mighty art of *printing with types*. He went to the grove and cut more letters; and then, using ink, pressed them upon a piece of parchment. He reversed the letters, and now they appeared properly placed upon the page. Then he formed words, and printed them also in the same way. He next cut the letters, no longer from the fragile bark, but from the solid wood. He managed to invent a thicker, glutinous ink, which would not blur the page when impressed on the parchment. Then he cut his letters out of lead, and finally out of pewter.

When his ignorant and superstitious neighbors heard what he was doing, some of them declared that he was a madman, while others darkly hinted that he was a sorcerer. After a while they annoyed him so much that he was forced to shut himself up and conceal his work from them ; and so he went on, month after month, striving to bring about the realization of the great art of printing, which he perceived to be possible.

One day, while old Coster was thus busily at work, a sturdy German youth, with a knapsack slung across his back, trudged into Haarlem. By some chance this youth happened to hear how the churchwarden was at work upon a wild scheme to print books instead of writing them. With beating heart the young man repaired to Coster's house, and made all haste to knock at the church-warden's humble door. Who this youth was, and what came of his visit to old Coster, will be told in the next chapter.

CHAPTER III

JOHN GUTENBERG, THE INVENTOR OF THE PRINTING-PRESS

THE sturdy young German who, with knap-sack on back and staff in hand, knocked at old Laurence Coster's door, was no ordinary youth. Although scarcely more than twenty, he had already seen a great deal of life, and even some of its rougher aspects.

John Gutenberg belonged to a family of high degree, and had been reared in such luxury as could be enjoyed in the rude mediæval time; but he did not allow luxuri-ous living to make him indolent or unam-bitious. He was an ardent student, and had received the best training which the learned monks could give him. Often, when a boy, he was found poring over the manuscripts

which he found in the monasteries where he
was educated.   He was also very religious in
thought and act.   Many a time he would
earnestly exclaim, what a pity it was that
the Bible was a closed book to the masses of
the people ;   that, as it was written by hand
on parchment, it could only be possessed
either by the churches and monasteries or by
very rich people.

Gutenberg's home was at Strasburg, on the
banks of the Rhine.   He had often dreamed
of foreign countries, and imagined what they
and their peoples were like ; so one day, being
strong of limb and active in exercise, he
resolved to pack up his knapsack, attire himself in walking costume, and take a long
pedestrian tour.   It was while on this jaunt
that, by a chance for which all later genera-
tions have had reason to be thankful, he
heard of old Coster and his discovery, and
hastened to present himself at the humble
churchwarden's door.

You can imagine the eagerness with which Coster led his young guest in, and how delighted he was to show him just how the printing of his letters worked. While with his rude leaden types the old man pressed letter after letter on the parchment, Gutenberg stood by, rapt in attention. Already he imagined that he saw dimly to what great uses this discovery might be put.

" And see here ! " exclaimed Coster, holding up some pages of parchment awkwardly sewed together, " *here is my first book in print.*"

It was a Latin grammar. Old Coster had slowly printed it, letter by letter, and right proud was he of this first triumph of his patient labor.

" But we can do better than this," said Gutenberg. " Your printing is even slower than the writing of the monks. From this day forth I will work upon this problem, and not rest till I have solved it."

Warmly grasping Coster's hand, and thank-
ing him for showing him his discovery,
Gutenberg resumed his knapsack, and trudged
out of Haarlem.   He had no longer any
thought of continuing his tramp into new
scenes.   His fondness for seeing strange lands
had for the while deserted him.   His only
thought was to get back as soon as possible
to Strasburg, where he lived, and to set to
work upon the task he had now set to himself.

Gutenberg lived in an age of dense superstition and ignorance.   Everything that was
new and unfamiliar seemed to the ignorant
people of that time to be the work of sorcery ;
and any one who dared to do things which
appeared marvellous in their eyes, was persecuted and pursued as if he dealt in evil magic.
No one knew this better than the young
Strasburg scholar.

So, on his arrival at Strasburg, he gave out
that he was at work making jewelry.   Mean-

while he locked himself up in his room, and, scarcely taking time to eat or sleep, devoted himself to the problem how to make Coster's discovery useful to the world. But he found that he was watched and interrupted, and that his hiding himself so constantly in his room gave rise to dark suspicions among his neighbors. So he repaired to an old ruined monastery, only one or two rooms of which were habitable, and which stood a few miles from the town. Here he thought he could work in peace, for the monastery ruin was in a lonely, deserted place.

Hidden in an obscure corner of this old monastery of St. Arbogaste was a little cell. This cell Gutenberg secured by a great oaken door with heavy bolts, and here he hid the tools and materials needed for his work. At the same time he fitted up a half-ruined room in a more open part of the monastery as a jewelry shop. He engaged two young men to help him polish precious stones and to repair trinkets. In this way he hoped to be able to work at his types in the hidden cell without discovery.

He now set to work, at such times as he could escape into his little cell, in dead earnest. It was not long before he had carved out of some bits of wood with his knife a number of separate types. The happy idea struck him to string these on a piece of wire in the form of words, and at last of sentences. Then, finding that wood was not hard enough, he carved some types, with more difficulty, in lead.

Having made types which satisfied him, Gutenberg used his knowledge of chemistry to make an ink which would leave a distinct imprint, and he soon succeeded in producing such an ink. As he continued to work, the great idea that was absorbing him grew more and more clear. He had his types and his ink, so he made a brush and a roller to put the ink on the types. He had now got as far

THE FIRST PRINTING-PRESS.   Page 39.

as printing a whole word or sentence on a piece of parchment; and by changing the movable types about, could form at will new words and sentences.

His next task was to construct "chases," so that the types could be held together, and would print in pages. And at last the idea of a *printing-press* was made a reality.

When Gutenberg had completed and gazed with delight on the first printing-press which had ever been constructed, the main difficulties of his task were over. With his types set in their chases, his different colored inks at his elbow, his rollers at hand to apply the ink, and his press ready to press the types down upon the blank pages, he stood ready to complete the first book printed with movable type.

But poor Gutenberg was not destined to derive much happiness from the results of his labors and the splendid invention he had made. He worked so hard that the few hours

of the night which he took for sleep were dis-
turbed by uneasy dreams. Sometimes he
thought that angelic voices warned him not
to go on with his printing, for that it would
bring untold miseries upon the human race.
Then he would rise in the morning, unre-
freshed by his slumbers and terrified by the
vision, and, seizing a mallet, would be on the
point of smashing his printing-press all to
pieces. But sometimes other spirits would
appear to him in dreams, and urge him to go
on with his good work, saying that it would
be an immense blessing and benefit to all the
world in all future ages. This would inspire
him with new energy, and he would toil the
next day with a light heart.

But after the printing-press had been made,
and he had really begun to print books, his
assistants in the jewelry shop betrayed him.
They told the magistrates of Strasburg about
his long absences and mysterious movements.
Their story soon spread through the town,

and roused the anger and hatred of the
writers of manuscript books, who feared lest
printing should ruin their occupation.

Gutenberg's enemies soon compelled him to
fly from Strasburg. He was stripped of all
he had in the world, and even his life was
threatened. So he went back to Mayence,
his birthplace, and there resumed his printing.
He took a rich jeweller, Fust, into partner-
ship. But he was not allowed to work long
in peace. Fust turned against him, and he
was soon forced to leave Mayence as he had
left Strasburg.

He was now wretchedly poor, and for a
while roamed aimlessly from place to place.
But at last he found a home in Nassau, the
ruler of which offered him his protection. In
that quiet town, Gutenberg set up his press
again, and printed many books, and spent the
remainder of his days, it is pleasant to say, in
rest, comfort and content, although he never
got rich from his invention. He died in the

year 1468, at the ripe age of sixty-nine; and many years after the statue of him, which may be seen standing in Mayence, was erected in his honor by the descendants of those who had driven him forth, a beggar, from his native city.

CHAPTER IV

PALISSY THE POTTER

IN the quaint old French village of Saintes there lived, more than three hundred years ago, a very strange, eccentric man.

So mysterious were his ways that his neighbors, who were simple, ignorant country folk, avoided and feared him. As he passed through the winding village street he was dressed so shabbily that he looked like a beggar. People who saw him for the first time half expected him to stop, put on a pleading face, and humbly ask for "one little sou."

Yet, threadbare as he was, his air was not at all that of a beggar. He hurried along with a brisk step. His large brown eyes glistened brightly, and there was almost always an eager smile upon his lips. He did not seem to be in the least conscious of his tatters; and if he nodded to his neighbors, and they turned their backs on him in reply, he went on smiling just as before.

This peculiar man dwelt in an old cottage a little out of the more thickly settled part of the village. He had a pale, thin, sad-looking wife, and three or four children, who looked as if they were far from being well fed. What was stranger still, he never liked to have any one enter his tumble-down cottage. It was clear to the village folk that he had some dark secret which he was very anxious to keep from all the world, and that he was afraid that if any one entered his door it would be discovered.

Those were very ignorant, superstitious times, and when there was a mystery about any one, it was always attributed to some wickedness or some unholy art. As this man passed a group of villagers, they would look

at him frowningly, and would fall to whisper-
ing to one another.

"He is a sorcerer," one would mutter,
"and makes witches' philters, and casts the
Evil One's spells over people."

"No," another one would say under his
breath; "he is a coiner of false money.
Look you: he has built a big furnace in the
back of his house, and he keeps it ever
a-roaring. You can see the smoke and
sparks shooting up any time o' day. There
he has his crucibles and chemical things,
and he carries his false pieces of money away
to the towns, and exchanges them for good,
honest ware."

Then perhaps a third, more kind-hearted
than the others, would reprove his comrades,
and, slowly shaking his head, would add:
"No, the poor wretch is mad—clean gone
mad. How else could the man, who is so
poor, in rags, with wife and children always
a-starving, go about with such bright eyes

and so brave an air ?   Be sure he is a madman.   God help his poor family ! "

But day after day the man went to and
fro, and heeded not his neighbors' frowns and
sneers, or their shrinking from him as he
passed by.

His name was Bernard Palissy, and his
whole soul was wrapped up in one object, to
which he sacrificed everything.

If you had entered the poor little cottage,
you would have indeed discovered just such
a furnace as the villager described; and
scattered about the room you would have
seen a number of pots, pieces of clay, and
various bottles and crucibles.   It was true,
too, that the furnace was always roaring
with a big fire, which was kept constantly
at red heat.

But Palissy was not a sorcerer, and was
not concocting any magic draught, or trying
to turn the baser metals into gold.   He was
engaged in a work which he knew, if he suc-

ceeded in it, would give him fame and wealth
to his heart's content.

Palissy, though of humble birth, had
picked up here and there a good deal of
knowledge of chemistry and the qualities of
minerals and ores.   He had, too, a very
ardent love of all beautiful objects.   He had
begun life as a surveyor, and had then
learned to paint on glass.   But though his
work was good, he did not succeed very well;
for, instead of attending to his business, he
was studying and dreaming his time away.

But an event happened one day which gave
him a new purpose in life, and changed the
whole current of his existence.   While wandering about a neighboring town he chanced
to spy in a shop window a very beautifully
decorated cup.   The fine polish and brilliant
colors of the cup at once attracted his artistic
eye; and, though he was poor, he managed
to scrape together enough money to buy it.

This cup, which had been made in Italy,

absorbed his attention.   He studied its every
line and feature, and kept wondering and
wondering how it received and could keep
such a beautiful, smooth, glossy polish.   No
such cup could ever have been made in
France.

What if *he* could find the way to make
beautiful ware like this!   Surely then his fortune would be made, and his poor wife would
wear Lyons silks, and his hungry little children would dine each day on ragoûts and the
best of fruits.

Palissy abandoned everything to achieve
this object which he now set before himself.
No more surveying or glass-painting for him.
He would discover for himself the art of
enamelling, or die in the attempt.

So, in the rear of his cottage, he built with
his own hands the big, rude furnace, bought
the chemicals which he thought necessary for
his work, collected a supply of the right kind
of clay, and resolutely set about his task.

For a long time he failed in every attempt to produce a bright enamel, such as he found on the Italian cup. Meanwhile, he grew poorer and poorer. His wife and children, poor things, scarcely got enough food to keep body and soul together.

One morning, when Palissy's hope was high that he would soon be able to perfect the enamel, a workman, whom he had hired for a pittance to help him, declared that he would not stay another day unless the money which was due him was paid. Palissy gave him his last suit of clothes; but the man was not satisfied, and soon went away. Left thus alone, Palissy worked with more desperate energy than ever. But now the wood which he used for the fuel of his furnace gave out, and he had no money to buy any more. All his labor seemed about to become in vain; for if the fire of the furnace went down, the enamel could not be made.

Stung almost into despair, Palissy was

struck by a sudden idea. He rushed into his little garden, tore down the trellises which supported his few fruit-trees and grape-vines, and hurled them on the fading fire. Yet, alas! the composition he had made and put into the furnace would not melt. The fire once more waned. Palissy then seized the chairs and tables, frantically broke them up, and cast them upon the flames. He tore the door from its hinges, the window-frames from their sockets, and piled them on the fire. Then seeing that the enamel did not yet melt, in his desperation he pulled up the very boards which formed the floor of the room, and added these to the roaring conflagration. As now he looked into the blazing fire, he of a sudden gave a wild shout of joy: "Come hither, good wife; come hither, my children!"

They hurried in, not knowing what to make of the frantic cry. As they entered the room where the furnace was, they saw Palissy, his face flushed with the heat, and

his eyes glistening with triumph, standing by
the furnace.   He held up the vase which he
had just taken from it.   It glittered with its
dazzling polish and its beautiful colors.   At
last he had indeed discovered the secret of
enamelling.   The time of triumph and fortune had come.

CHAPTER V

WILLIAM LEE, THE INVENTOR OF THE
STOCKING-FRAME

THOSE who have strolled through the streets of the old town of Cambridge, in England, will not easily forget the many college edifices which appear on every side, composing the ancient University. Many of these buildings are imposing and beautiful. They are adorned with numerous architectural devices : with arches, gables, oriel windows, gargoyles, pinnacles, and other sculptural ornaments, and almost all of them bear the marks of great age. The air of the town is one of studious repose; it seems a place well fitted for quiet study and for the pursuits of tranquil scholars. The old town has changed so little, moreover, in the progress of time, that very much as it looks now it looked in the good Queen Elizabeth's time, three centuries ago.

It was in the reign of Elizabeth that a young man named William Lee repaired to Cambridge to get an university education. Lee was a country lad who had been brought up on a large farm. From childhood he had been fond of study, and had had a craving for knowledge. He loved reading and learning far better than the active duties on his father's farm. All the time he was at the University he studied hard, and at the end of his course had taken a high rank among his comrades. As a reward for his good scholarship he was given a " Fellowship." This provided him with a small income, and enabled him to continue living at the University after graduating, still pursuing his studies there.

Lee was one of those dreamy, thoughtful young men who care for little outside of their books, and, being much wrapped up in them,

learn but little of the ways of the busy world.
He was not in the least what we call a
"practical man." His life was absorbed in
the love and pursuit of book knowledge. He
was wholly unfitted for any other kind of
work. His destiny seemed to be to live and
die a college professor.

And so he might have done if his fate had
not led him astray into the paths of love. If
he had not fallen in love, probably the world
never would have heard of William Lee. He
was fond of wandering through the pretty
roads and hedge-bound lanes in the vicinity
of Cambridge, taking a book with him on his
jaunts, and sauntering dreamily along the
paths, thinking of what he had been reading.

It chanced that on one of these excursions
he met a young country lass with such rosy
cheeks and bright eyes that he was at once
roused out of his reverie and attracted to her.
His dreams now took another turn. He
thought less of his books, and more of the

maiden who had stirred his heart. She lived on a poor little farm some miles away from the town ; and Lee, having succeeded in making her acquaintance, betook himself more and more often to the modest cottage where she dwelt. To his delight, his affection was soon returned; and now many were the happy hours which he spent at his rosy-cheeked young lady-love's side. But there was one drawback to his pleasure, which greatly worried him. The young girl's parents were very poor, and it was her task to eke out the small family income by knitting stockings. She had her household duties to perform during the day, and so she was obliged to take up her knitting in the evenings. Oftentimes when Lee came she was so busy with her work that she could not talk to him.

At last his patience was exhausted, and he proposed that they should get married. He thought that his income as a " Fellow " would suffice for both, and he would be care-

ful to keep his marriage secret. It was a law
of the University that the Fellows should be
unmarried men, and Lee saw that if his marriage were known he would lose his Fellowship and be thrown upon the world.

So one morning they got married. But
Lee's happiness was not long-enduring. His
marriage was soon discovered, and he was
abruptly expelled from his Fellowship in the
University. Worse still, when his father
heard of the marriage, he disowned poor
William, who was now cast upon the world
with his young wife without a penny. What
should they do? If they did not go to work,
they must soon starve. Every day they grew
poorer and more wretched.

His young wife, who was very cheerful and
industrious, took up her knitting once more,
in order to earn enough, if possible, to support them. As for poor Lee, he was totally
unfitted to do anything, and his pride was
greatly hurt to sit idly by while his wife

toiled patiently, hour after hour, on her work.

One day, as he sat watching her fingers busily plying the needles, a bright thought suddenly struck him. Could not a machine be somehow contrived which, imitating human fingers, would knit stockings? If he could only devise such a machine, his wife would no longer have to work so hard, and perhaps it might even bring fortune to his poverty-stricken door. It seemed that there was something practical in the poor student after all. He set eagerly to work to realize his new idea. He studied such machines as he could find in his neighborhood. He made a great number of models, and was not disheartened when one after another failed to perform the task he had in view. But at last the day came when an actual working *stocking-frame* stood in the miserable little room which was all the home he had. He had successfully carried out the idea of imitating fingers knitting, and to his joy he found himself now able to weave stockings on his machine finer in texture, and more rapidly, than those which were made with his wife's hands.

It was not long before Lee's great invention became known far and wide. Queen Elizabeth heard of the silk stockings woven by Lee's frame, and, having received a pair, vowed that she would never wear cloth hose any more, but would always thereafter wear woven silk stockings. The great ladies adopted the fashion, and Lee found himself raised at last above the galling poverty which he had suffered after his marriage. He established himself at Calverton, not far from his native place, and for some time he did a thriving business. But so valuable was his machine that pretty soon unscrupulous men began to make machines like it, and so Lee lost much of the benefit of his invention. Though the proud Elizabeth was glad enough to wear the fine silk stockings, she would not protect him against those who invaded his rights, and when King James came to the throne he also refused to aid the inventor.

But Lee, who had proved himself a far more energetic and able man than he had seemed to be in his studious days, was resolved that he would continue the industry which he had created. So he packed up his machines and crossed over to France. There he was heartily welcomed by the great-hearted King Henry the Fourth, and by Sully, the king's wise and far-seeing minister. Lee settled in the beautiful old town of Rouen, where he became so busy that he employed nine men to help him weave stockings. His wife could now sit at home at ease and take care of their children. Happy days had dawned upon them, and it seemed as if their troubles had forever vanished.

One day, however, the good king who had so generously befriended the English inventor

was murdered as he was riding in his car-
riage. Lee was now forced to give up his
establishment at Rouen, and sought obscurity
and safety in Paris. There, it is said, he died
in poverty and wretchedness before he had
passed the middle years of life. Some of his
workmen returned to England, and one of his
apprentices, named Aston, set up a stocking
factory in his own country, and established
the weaving of stockings as a permanent
industry of England. Thus Lee's invention
proved to be of the greatest benefit to his
native land, although he himself did not reap
fortune from it.

But happily his name was not forgotten.
Some time after his death a curious painting
was made of him watching his wife at her
knitting. He was represented as wearing the
costume of his college, and pointing to an
iron stocking-frame, while his wife was busy
with her needles at his side. On the picture
was this quaint inscription: "In the year

1589 the ingenious William Lee, of St. John's
College, Cambridge, devised this profitable
art for stockings (but, being despised, went
to France); yet of iron to himself, but to us
and to others of gold; in memory of whom
this is here painted." The curious old picture
long hung in the Stocking-weavers' Hall, in
London, but has now disappeared.

So lived, loved, worked, and died the
modest scholar who gave to England one of
her greatest industries, to create which he
was inspired by his tender affection for his
wife.

CHAPTER VI

THE BUILDERS OF THE EDDYSTONE

AMONG the world's greatest benefactors have been the patient and heroic men who, often at the peril of life, have reared light-houses on dangerous reefs. The lighthouse, standing lonely, quiet, and ever steadfast amid the restive turbulence of the sea, serves two useful purposes. It warns away the tempest-tossed sailor from the crags on which it stands, and it guides him toward the safe havens on the shore. Thus it converts what was once a perpetual danger of the ocean into an actual means of security and life.

For many a century, a certain jagged reef of rocks which lies about twelve miles off the English coast, in the rough English Channel, was a terror to all the seamen who approached it. Many a goodly craft had struck upon its jutting crags, and had in an instant broken up and sunk to the bottom. Often hidden amid dense fogs, the ships of the olden time could never make out just where it lay; and each year it claimed and devoured its victims, sometimes by the hundred, so that those near and dear to them never knew what had been their fate.

The ocean, dashing in ceaseless breakers upon this hideous mass of rocks, breaks in circling eddies and whirlpools around them; and from this circumstance the reef, ages ago, received the now famous name of the Eddystone.

It was upon this terrible reef of the Eddystone that the first lighthouse which was ever built upon a rock at a distance from the mainland was erected; and it is curious that the idea of putting a lighthouse there was conceived, not by a sailor or an engineer, not

by a man of science or by the government,
but by a quiet, eccentric English country
gentleman.   About two centuries ago this
gentleman, whose name was Henry Winstanley, was living at ease in his ancient manor-
house in eastern England.   Winstanley was
a very queer, whimsical man.   He was quite
rich, and used his wealth in a very singular
way.   His neighbors, though they liked him
for his good-nature and easy-going ways,
thought that he was perhaps a little
"cracked."   Winstanley, among other odd
traits, was very fond of playing practical
jokes.   Indeed, he spent a good deal of his
time and money in giving people sudden
shocks and surprises.   He filled his house
and grounds, for instance, with all sorts of
strange devices for this purpose.

Yet it was this very man of strange whims
and terrifying jokes, Henry Winstanley, who
undertook the unheard-of feat of erecting a
lighthouse on the tempest-riven reef of the

Eddystone.   Inspired by the noble idea of
saving so many lives and so much property
from the jaws of the great deep, Winstanley
abandoned his idle life and went to work
with a will.   He himself aided and superin-
tended his workmen, giving up all his time
and energies to the great work.   For six
years he toiled ceaselessly to finish it.   He
constantly braved the storms that ever swept
around the dreadful reef ; more than once,
bound to the rock, he came near starving ;
and when the lighthouse had been reared,
and was all but completed, he fell at last a
victim to his noble design.

One evening at dusk, Winstanley, with a
party of his workmen, set out in a boat from
Plymouth to put some finishing touches to
the lighthouse.   Just as he was starting, a
friend, pointing to the gathering clouds,
warned him that a storm was brewing, and
begged him not to go.   But Winstanley,
in his reckless way, replied, " I only wish I

could be at the lighthouse in the greatest storm that ever blew under the face of the heavens." His wish was to be fulfilled sooner than he thought. As night closed in, the tower of the lighthouse could be dimly seen from the shore, rising proudly above the angry surge. But before the next morning dawned it had disappeared forever from human sight. The crags of the Eddystone rose grim, bleak, and bare from the swelling bosom of the sea. The brave Winstanley and all his men, and every stone, and buttress, and cable, and nail of his lighthouse — everything excepting only a single chain which remained riveted in the crevice of the rock — had been swept away. For all had gone down under the most terrific gale which had raged in the English Channel for many years.

But the sad fate of Winstanley did not prevent other intrepid spirits from making fresh attempts to transform the Eddystone from an awful peril into a beacon of safety.

Four years after Winstanley was lost, a plain, sensible man, John Rudyerd, whose trade was to deal in silk goods, went to work and erected a wooden lighthouse, which was shaped like a pine cone, on the bleak and barren reef. But as the waters and winds had proved the destruction of Winstanley's tower, so fire afterward consumed that of Rudyerd.

Rudyerd's tower stood the brunt of wave and storm for forty-six years. Then, early one cold December morning, some fishermen, who were getting ready their nets on the beach, saw clouds of smoke issuing from the lighthouse. Three men were known to be in the lighthouse; one of them, the keeper, was ninety-four years old. As soon as these men discovered the fire, they began to work frantically with their buckets; but their water was soon exhausted. They became wild with fright, and the terrible heat soon exhausted them. The melting lead, too, began to drop

on them from the roof, and burned them
terribly. As the flames spread through the
tower, and swept down with fierce rapidity
from the top to the bottom, the terror-
stricken men retreated before it until they
sought refuge from the blazing beams and
molten lead in a big crevice in the rock.
There they huddled together, almost dead
with terror and pain.

Meanwhile the fishermen on shore had
jumped into a boat, and had rowed with
might and main to the crag. They arrived
just in time to save the poor wretches from
being burned. Their sufferings had been
terrible. No sooner had the boat brought
them safely to the shore than one of them,
the moment he got out of the boat, was seized
with an insane frenzy. He plunged into the
forest and was never more seen. As for the
poor old keeper, he was so entirely overcome
by his fright and his maddening burns, that
he died a few days after his rescue.

THE EDDYSTONE LIGHTHOUSE. Page 69.

The third Eddystone Lighthouse, which stood sturdily on the rock for more than a hundred years, was erected four years after Rudyerd's tower was burned. It was built by John Smeaton, one of the greatest inventors and engineers of the eighteenth century.

It is said that, when a small boy, Smeaton liked to play with workmen's tools rather than with children's ordinary toys. At the early age of fourteen he built an engine for turning rose-work, and at twenty-five he invented an instrument for measuring a ship's way at sea.

The lighthouse which Smeaton erected on the tempest-beaten crag of the Eddystone was a noble column of granite, which rose to a height of eighty-five feet. It resembled in shape the trunk of an oak-tree, and swept up in a gentle curve from its base. On the summit was placed a large lantern, with a gallery around it. This famous lighthouse was taken down, stone by stone, in 1884, and re-erected on a height on the mainland, near the old seafaring town of Plymouth — on the very spot, indeed, where Queen Elizabeth's brave old sea-warriors, Drake, Hawkins, and Frobisher, were playing their famous game of bowls, three hundred years ago, when the Spanish Armada hove in sight in the English Channel. A new and larger lighthouse was built on the Eddystone; and this it is which to-day sheds its far-gleaming rays over the waters, and guides the sailors to their homes on the shore.

CHAPTER VII

THE INVENTORS OF COTTON-MACHINERY :
KAY ; HARGREAVES ; ARKWRIGHT

THE machinery for the spinning of cotton yarn, and for the weaving and printing of cotton cloths, has, in every part of it, been invented and brought to its present excellence within the past one hundred and fifty years. As lately as in 1730, no machine whatever existed even for the spinning of yarn.

To six men of genius especially — five Englishmen and one American — is to be awarded the distinction of having established the cotton manufacture as one of the mightiest of the world's industries. For this industry has, in a century, created the English Manchester out of a straggling rural hamlet, and Liverpool out of an obscure fishing village ;

has transformed the English county of Lancaster from a dreary and barren waste into a noisy network of dense, busy towns and crowded factories.

These six men were John Kay, who invented the fly-shuttle; James Hargreaves, who devised the spinning-jenny; Richard Arkwright, who made the water frame; Samuel Crompton, who constructed the spinning-mule; Edmund Cartwright, whose genius produced the power-loom; and Eli Whitney, to whom we owe the great improvement of the cotton gin.

Down to a period as recent as 1730, the spinning of cotton yarn was done by the finger and thumb, a thread at a time. The yarn was also woven by hand, the shuttle being thrown back by each hand alternately. It was in 1733 that John Kay revolutionized the art of weaving by introducing his fly-shuttle.

This machine, which seems simple even to

uncouthness to our eyes, merely supplied a handle and spring, with which the shuttle could be worked with one hand. But so important was the change which the fly-shuttle effected, that Kay became at once the object of persecution by two opposite classes.

The weavers, on one hand, were so incensed that they burst into his house, destroyed every one of his machines on which they could lay their hands, and threatened him with the same furious treatment. The capitalists, on the other hand, welcomed his invention. But they attempted to use it without right, and to deprive him of all the benefits of his device. Kay was forced to take refuge in Paris, where he soon after died in beggary and neglect.

A fate scarcely less harsh overtook the next great improver of cotton machinery. James Hargreaves was a poor but ingenious weaver. A sore need was felt for some device which would spin yarn more rapidly than had before been done.

One day, an accident revealed to Hargreaves how this could be effected. As he sat brooding in his humble cottage, his wife's spinning-wheel happened to fall over upon the floor. Hargreaves perceived that the wheel still continued to revolve, the spindle being now in an upright, instead of a horizontal position.

This gave him the hint which he needed. He went to work and made a spinning-frame, with eight spindles and a horizontal wheel. This machine he called after his wife (Jenny) the "spinning-jenny." But no sooner had his invention become known to the neighboring spinners, than Hargreaves was assailed by a storm of savage anger and abuse.

His cottage was attacked by a brutal mob. His precious spinning-jenny was broken to atoms; and he himself barely escaped, with his wife, from the eager clutches of his enemies.

HARGREAVES'S SPINNING-JENNY.   Page 74.

The rest of his life, like that of Kay before him, was a dreary yet patient struggle against starvation ; and he, too, died unacknowledged, poor, an outcast, his invention having proved the greatest misfortune of his life.

One of the most prosperous and busy towns in the great manufacturing region in northern England is Bolton. A hundred and thirty years ago it was a much smaller town than now, but it had then the reputation of being one of England's most thriving industrial centres. At that time Bolton was a queer straggling place, with many old grimy houses, and many narrow lanes and alleys branching off from the streets. One of these alleys conducted the wayfarer to an ancient, cosey inn, the Old Millstone. If you had been walking in this alley about the year 1750, you would have seen a rude sign hanging over a cellar on one side, bearing these words : " Come to the underground Barber ! He shaves for a penny !"

Descending into the cellar, you would have found the barber to be a bright-eyed, active, keen-looking young man about twenty-one years of age, standing ready in his shirt-sleeves to shave the next customer. Nor would he have to wait long, for the cheap rate at which he relieved people of their stubby beards brought an almost continual succession of artisans from the neighboring machine-shops to his dark little cellar.

When he had shaved a customer, the latter would hasten to a lead cistern against the wall to wash his face ; for barbers in those days did not "fix up" their customers as comfortably after shaving as they do now.

This lively barber, besides being very expert at his trade, was, like many another barber before him and since, a great talker. Everybody who came under the swift sweep of his razor had to pay his contribution of chatter. The barber asked his customers about their various trades, and he was always especially eager to learn what anybody would tell him about machinery. He loved to hear all about the new machines which were introduced from time to time into the shops and factories — how they were made, how they worked, how much labor they saved, and what kind of goods they turned out.

The name of our inquisitive and energetic barber was Richard Arkwright. His childhood and boyhood had not been very happy. His father was a very poor man, and had thirteen children. Of course, as there were then no free schools in England, he could not hope to give this large family a good education. The result was that Richard grew up without learning much of anything, and just as soon as he was strong enough to work he was set about it. Yet Richard was a youth of a very persevering, resolute spirit. He had a manly independence about him and a cheerful courage, which enabled him to bear bravely whatever hardships came upon him, and to sturdily carry on his struggles with the world.

While he was shaving for a penny, he was always dreaming of something better and more profitable. He knew that he had a good deal of mechanical ingenuity, and he resolved to put it to use as soon as he could. He spent the little leisure time he had in studying machinery, and in trying to invent something. By the time he was thirty, Richard made up his mind that he had had quite enough of the shaving business. He worked hard, yet he only made enough to keep body and soul together; he was laying up nothing for the future. So, throwing aside the razor, he took up the trade of a dealer in hair.

He wandered about the country, buying the ringlets of rustic young girls, making them up into wigs, and selling them to the old people. Meanwhile he invented a new way of dyeing hair, which brought him in quite a brisk

trade.   He thrived so well in his new business that he laid up a considerable sum of
money, and falling in love with a farmer's
daughter, he married her.

One day he was in a manufacturing town,
where he heard some weavers talking about
the threads used in the weaving of cloth.
The cloth they made consisted of linen thread
woven with cotton.   But it was hard, they
said, to get enough cotton thread to form
what was called the "weft" of the cloth.   A
machine for spinning cotton thread had
already been invented by the poor weaver,
James Hargreaves, to whom his invention
had been nothing but a misfortune, since
he had been persecuted and driven from
place to place, because the spinners thought
that his "spinning-jenny" would deprive them
of work.   But the spinning-jenny did not produce enough thread for the demand, nor was
its thread fine and close enough for the weft.

Richard Arkwright listened intently to all

that the weavers were saying. He plied them with questions. He found one of Hargreaves's spinning-jennies, and examined closely its every part. From that time he had but one idea — to invent a machine which would spin thread faster and finer than the spinning-jenny. And now, like many inventors who absorb themselves in their one idea, Richard began to neglect his regular business. His young wife was angry to see him daily growing poorer and poorer; for, instead of saving money, he did not now earn enough to give them the common comforts of life. Instead of going up and down the country for his stock of maidens' tresses, he stayed at home, making models of machines and brooding over them by the hour together. One day he would feel sure that the model he had just made would answer the purpose, and bring fame and fortune at last; the next, he would discover some fatal defect, would throw the model aside, and begin on a new one.

They finally grew so poor that it was hard
for them to procure enough to eat from
day to day.   Richard's wife, who was a
young woman of rather violent temper, was
always upbraiding him for what she thought
his idleness, and crying out to him that his
attempts to invent a spinning-machine were
all nonsense.   At last her patience gave way
entirely, and one day she seized the last
model, which he had carefully and laboriously
made, and in a fit of rage threw it violently
on the floor.

Richard could not stand this.   He was
infuriated to see his pretty model lying on
the floor in twenty pieces, and told his wife
to leave him forever.   She obeyed him, going
away from their humble home, never to
return.

After several years of great poverty and
suffering, during which he met and overcame
many obstacles, Richard at last completed the
machine which has made his name immortal

in the annals of invention. It was while he
was struggling with his troubles that one day
he arrived at Preston, which he had made his
home.   An election for member of Parliament was going on, and his vote was greatly
needed. But he looked so shabby and ragged
that the party managers were ashamed to
lead him to the polls. So they took him to
a tailor's, fitted him out with a new suit of
clothes, and brought him up to the voting-
place.

But the old days of want vanished
forever after Arkwright had at last introduced his spinning-frame.   This machine
produced a cotton thread fit not only for the
" weft," but also for the " warp " of the cloth,
so that the cloth could now be woven wholly
of cotton.

In a few years the beautiful vale of the
river Derwent, in the centre of England,
revealed to the eye several large mills busily
at work with Arkwright's machines, and not

far from them rose a stately country-house,
with parks and lawns, known as Willersley
Castle.   Both the mills and the castle belonged
to Richard Arkwright, who had become rich
and prosperous, and was growing richer every
day.

He who had once been a humble barber in
a dingy cellar, shaving workmen for a penny
apiece, was now one of the chief men of his
neighborhood, and one of the most famous in
all England.   He was made High Sheriff of
his county, which in England is a high honor;
and once, when King George the Third paid
a visit to the locality, Arkwright, as Sheriff,
presented the monarch with an address of wel-
come.   For this slight deed, and not because
he was the inventor of one of the most useful
machines ever made, the king made Arkwright
a knight, so that he rose from his knees with the
title of Sir Richard Arkwright.   Thus titled,
rich, and renowned, the inventor lived to a
good old age, happy in the respect of all men.

CHAPTER VIII

THE INVENTORS OF COTTON-MACHINERY, CONTINUED: CROMPTON, CARTWRIGHT, WHITNEY

THE next advance in cotton machinery was the spinning-mule, invented by the shy, simple, and confiding Samuel Crompton. Crompton's mule is confidently declared to be "the fulcrum of that mighty lever, the cotton trade of England." It almost displaced the spinning-jenny of Hargreaves, and its principle has remained to this day, for the most part, unchanged.

It may be fairly said that it was Samuel Crompton, chiefly, who created by his invention that great network of English manufacturing towns, of which the centre is Blackburn; which includes Oldham, Preston, and Manchester; and to which appears to have been awarded the special task of clothing mankind.

Crompton revealed the signs of unusual talents at a very early age. He was fond of books. He had a rare taste for music. He constructed excellent fiddles when a mere boy. He early learned to weave, and before he had arrived at manhood had already begun to construct, in his own mind, the machine which was destined, not indeed to enrich him, but to add enormously to the wealth and prosperity of his native country.

In the "Hall-in-the-Wood," an ancient, rambling mansion which stood amid fine old oaks on the banks of the river Eagley, near Bolton, Crompton worked diligently and in secret for five years. At the end of that time, the spinning-mule had grown into a practical machine. It united the leading features of the machines of Hargreaves and Arkwright, and turned out a yarn easily superior to anything previously produced.

But now Crompton was called upon to undergo the same persecutions and bitter wrongs which had assailed the others. The same Blackburn weavers and spinners who had driven Hargreaves from his home now attacked Crompton, and destroyed his machines. He took one of his mules to pieces, and hid it in the roof of the "Hall-in-the-Wood." When, after many weeks, the rage of his enemies subsided, he put the mule together again, and, hid in the garret, spun his yarn upon it day and night.

Soon the yarn which he produced became famous for its firmness and fineness through all the country round. Curious folk flocked from every direction to see his machine. When Crompton refused them admission, they brought ladders, and climbed up to the windows to catch a glimpse of it. "One pertinacious fellow," so goes the story, "hid himself for several days in the cock-loft, from which he watched Crompton at work in the garret below, through a gimlet hole which he had bored in the ceiling."

Crompton's struggles against poverty, mob-violence, and many attempted thefts of his invention, were long and desperate; but he bore them all with a sweet and patient temper, which showed him to be a hero among men.

After many years of suspense, however, he seemed at last to be on the very verge of receiving the reward of his splendid service to the great industry of cotton-spinning. The prime minister of England, Spencer Perceval, expressed his intention of conferring on the veteran inventor a liberal pension.

One day, Crompton was awaiting the prime minister in the lobby of the House of Commons. Presently Perceval came up and told Crompton that he should receive twenty thousand pounds, as a gift from the nation. Perceval then turned away to enter the House. At that instant the sharp ring of a pistol

echoed through the hall.   There was a loud
cry of alarm and dismay.   Perceval fell to the
floor, shot through the heart by the crazy
assassin Bellingham.   Crompton's last hope
was gone, and he turned sadly away.   The
man who had created a machine which even
then spun daily a thousand pounds of yarn,
was put off with a pittance of five thousand
pounds, which was at once swallowed up by
his debts; and Crompton, like Kay and Hargreaves before him, spent the days of his old
age in privation, neglect, and almost in
beggary.

The four men who have already been
described as the pioneers in the invention of
cotton machinery were all of humble origin.
They were what we are wont to call self-
made men.   Kay was an artisan loom-maker,
Arkwright was a barber and then a dealer in
hair, Hargreaves and Crompton were obscure
weavers.   Each, by the sheer force of un-
tutored genius, rose from the lower regions of

hand-labor, into the higher sphere of success-- ful inventors.

The next in the line of cotton-machine inventors, however, was a man of far dif- ferent pursuits. Edmund Cartwright came of an excellent family. He was a graduate of the University of Oxford. He was a quiet country clergyman of the Church of England. He was a man of tranquil literary tastes, a student, a bookworm, and a tolerable poet. Nothing, it would seem, could be more remote from the bent of his mind than mechanics. His habits were all those of the study, and of the even tenor of pious duty.

In this quiet and useful life, Cartwright lived on to middle age. It was not until his fortieth year that, strangely and suddenly, the genius of mechanical invention awoke within him. A chance conversation at the dinner table led to the great invention by Edmund Cartwright of the power-loom.

It appeared that Arkwright's machines

were spinning more yarn than the weavers
could turn into cloth. It struck the grave
country parson, Cartwright, that machinery
might be devised which would weave the
yarn as fast as it could be spun. His com-
panions at table ridiculed the idea as absurd ;
but Cartwright retorted that he had just seen,
in London, a curious automaton figure which
moved chessmen to their proper places on the
chessboard, for all the world as if it were
alive.

"Before many years," declared the learned
churchman, "we shall have weaving Johnnies,
as well as spinning Jennies."

He himself fulfilled his daring prophecy.
He had never seen a loom in his life; but
from this time forth he brooded perpetually
upon the idea which floated, at first vaguely
and then more and more definitely, in his
mind. It is to be feared that the church
fairs, the parish children, and the pastoral
visits were somewhat neglected ; that the

doctor's favorite poets and essayists took on layers of dust, and that the doctor's sermons were somewhat less edifying than of old.

" He was often observed by his family," says his biographer, " striding up and down the room in a fit of abstraction, and throwing his arms violently from side to side, like a weaver jerking the shuttles."

After months of thought and repeated experiment, the power-loom was completed as a practical machine, and it soon brought about a complete revolution in the weaving of cotton cloths.

But neither Cartwright's age, nor sacred calling, nor immense service to the industries of England, saved him from persecution, or sheltered him from the biting cares of poverty. Masters and men were up in arms against him as soon as his design was known. His goods were maliciously damaged; his workmen were spirited away from him; his patent right was repeatedly infringed. Calumny and hatred dogged his steps.

After a succession of disasters his prospects assumed a brighter hue. A large Manchester firm contracted for the use of four hundred looms. But a few days after they were at work, the mill which had been built to receive them stood a heap of blackened ruins.

When Cartwright had turned from his quiet pastoral pursuits to the labors of invention, he had been the possessor of a large fortune. He was now so reduced in means, that, in his old age, he was forced to attempt to gain a bare living by his pen. But soon the fascination of inventing drew him again irresistibly into the troublous field from which he had been driven by poverty. He had not entered it at first for the sake of riches.

Cartwright was a man of a singularly noble, benevolent, unselfish character. His high purpose was to benefit mankind ; and to that purpose he clung with heroic fidelity.

Neither discouragement nor ruin could cow him, or drive him from it. So it was that the years of his old age, spent though they mostly were in privation, were filled with varied and useful labors. The resources of his inventive genius seemed unlimited. He devised wool-combing machines, and baking machines; rope-making machines and fire preventives; ploughs and wheel-carriages. He had, too, that wonderful foresight which has so often been a gift of men of inventive genius; for, twenty years before Fulton piloted the " Clermont " up the Hudson, Cartwright predicted to his son that, if he lived to be a man, he would see both ships and land-carriages impelled by steam.

Eli Whitney was one of those bright, precocious Yankee boys who in early years reveal a great fondness for making things, and who show ingenuity in doing whatever they turn their hands to. His father was a plain Massachusetts farmer, who tilled his

acres near Westborough in that State. Eli,
from the first, disliked farming. He avoided
farm work whenever he could, and instead
spent much of his time in his father's workshop. The good farmer was in the habit of
repairing his own wheels and chairs and
mending his fences, so that he had a small
collection of tools. These tools were Eli's
delight. Whenever he had the chance he
would slip away into the workshop and try
to fashion some article which his already ingenious mind had designed.

On one occasion, when Eli was twelve
years old, his father, on his return from a
journey, asked what his boys had been doing
during his absence. The reply was that the
other boys had been steadily at work in the
fields, but that Eli had spent his time in
the workshop.

" And what has he been doing there ? "

" He has been making a fiddle."

" Ah," sighed the worthy farmer, " I

fear Eli will have to take his portion in fiddles!"

Nevertheless, the fiddle proved to be a very good one, and served its purpose quite well at the country dances in the neighborhood.

Another time the farmer, on going to church one Sunday morning, chanced to leave his watch — a big, old-fashioned silver "turnip" — at home. As soon as his father was out of the house, Eli seized the watch, and eagerly took it to pieces, bit by bit. When he saw what he had done he was horrified, for his father was a very strict man, and would be sure to punish him severely for spoiling his watch. So Eli set to work, and by dint of his skill succeeded in putting the watch together again just as the farmer got back from church. So neatly did he do this that his father never discovered how his watch had been treated, until, years after, Eli told him what he had done.

There are many other stories of Eli's

youthful ingenuity, which there is not space
to repeat here. He was always trying his
hand at something, and he usually succeeded
in whatever he attempted. His stepmother
found him useful in a hundred ways in the
household, repairing old utensils and making
new ones. When the Revolutionary War
broke out, Eli began to make nails, which
were greatly needed by the patriots. Then
he turned his hand to making the long pins
which the women of that day used for fas-
tening their bonnets; and he also for a while
drove a thriving trade in walking-sticks, in
which he invented many striking and graceful devices.

As Eli approached manhood he began to
feel sorely the need of a better education
than the country schools afforded. He had
studied much by himself in the intervals
between work, and knew more about mathematics and mechanics than most lads of his
age. But he was not satisfied with this. He

wanted to go to college. His father was resolutely opposed to this, and refused to give him the means. So Eli set hard to work, and managed, by making various articles and teaching school, to save enough money to enter college. He went to Yale when he was twenty-three years old, and graduated four years later. While in college young Whitney gave many proofs of his mechanical ingenuity. On one occasion he repaired the apparatus of one of the professors, who was about to send it to Europe for the purpose, as he supposed that no one in this country had the skill to do it.

Eli Whitney at first intended to adopt teaching as his profession. His heart was wrapped up in mechanics, but he was poor, and could see no way in which he could follow his natural bent. Not long after graduating, therefore, he accepted an engagement as a tutor in the family of a gentleman who lived in Georgia. It was a fortunate accident that, while on his way to the South, young Whitney made the acquaintance of the widow of the famous Revolutionary hero, General Nathaniel Greene. This lady, who lived near Savannah, at once took a liking to him, and on their arrival in Georgia invited him to stay for a while at her home. This was all the more agreeable, as Whitney found, to his disappointment, that the gentleman who had engaged him had selected another tutor. Mrs. Greene kindly cheered him, and told him to make her house his home.

Thus left without the employment which had been promised him, Whitney again turned his attention to his first love, mechanics. It happened that an occasion soon arose when he was able to show his generous hostess and friend how skilful he was in mechanical devices. The good lady was fond of embroidery, but found that the tambour or frame upon which she did her delicate work was not well fitted for that purpose. Whitney eagerly assured her that he could make a frame which would serve her much better. He set cheerfully to work, and had soon completed a frame far superior to the old one.

This proof of his inventive talent greatly impressed Mrs. Greene, and soon opened to the young man the grand opportunity of his life. Not long after, Mrs. Greene was entertaining a number of her husband's old army friends at Mulberry Grove, her home. One day the conversation happened to turn upon the cotton production of the Southern States. One of the officers remarked that cotton could be easily raised all through the South, but that so long as it required so much labor to separate the cotton from its seed, the cotton crop could not be made a profitable one. If any device could be found, he added, by which the cotton could be easily cleaned, the production of cotton would become an enormously paying industry.

"Gentlemen," said Mrs. Greene, who was intently listening to the talk, "tell this to my young friend, Mr. Whitney. I verily believe he can make anything."

Now Whitney had never seen a piece of cotton in his life; none the less, he promptly made up his mind that he would devote his every energy to solving the problem thus put to him. He first examined some cotton, and saw at once what the task was which he had to perform. He had no tools with which to begin his work, but he sturdily set about making some.

In less than ten days he had completed his first model of a cotton-cleaning machine. He was delighted with its success, and went on improving it by every device he could think of. In two or three months he had perfected a perfectly practicable working *cotton-gin*. It was speedily proved that this machine, which could be worked by a single man or woman, could clean more cotton in a single day than could be done by a man or woman, by the old hand method, in several months. The immense utility of the cotton-gin was at once recognized throughout the South; and now Whitney suffered, as so many inventors had suffered before him, from the dishonesty of greedy money-makers. The building in which his cotton-gin was kept was broken into, and the cotton-gin taken away. It was at once copied, and put into use in various places before he could get his patent.

The fruits of his great invention were thus stolen from him. Although he got several patents, he never grew rich, as so many Southern planters did by the use of his machine. In vain he petitioned Congress for redress and compensation. The inventor of the cotton-gin, by which he undoubtedly created the wealth and power of nearly every Southern State, lived and died almost in a state of poverty. But his was a patient and heroic spirit. He bore the injustice of men and the ingratitude of his country with cheerful serenity, and died assured at least of a deathless fame, with his name enrolled high up on the list of the world's greatest inventors.

CHAPTER IX

JAMES WATT, THE INVENTOR OF THE STEAM-ENGINE

IN a small cottage at Greenock, near Glasgow, in Scotland, there was living, about a century and a half ago, a very bright but delicate boy. In many ways he was quite unlike other boys of his age. He was very fond of books, yet he disliked going to school so much that, being feeble in health, his parents kept him at home. He was a very truthful boy. When any dispute took place between him and his playmates, his father would always say, " Let us hear what James says about it. From him I always get the truth."

When this boy was seven or eight years old a neighbor said to his father, " Why don't you send this lad to school? He is wasting his time doing nothing here at home."

"See what he is doing," was the father's reply, "before you say he is wasting his time."

The neighbor looked down at James, who was seated on the hearth. He was not amusing himself with playthings, but was very busy drawing triangles and curves and other mathematical lines. "You must pardon my hasty words," said the neighbor; "his education has not been neglected; he is, indeed, no common child."

Not far away from his own home lived an aunt of James, with whom he often stayed. One day, the aunt found him in the kitchen, studying her tea-kettle. He was bent over it, and was closely watching the steam which puffed from its spout. Then he would take off the lid, hold a cup over the steam, and carefully count the drops of water into which it was condensed. The aunt roundly scolded

him for what she thought his trifling. She
little dreamed that the boy was taking his
first lesson in a science, by the pursuit of
which he was destined to change the whole
character of the industries of the world, and
win for himself an immortal fame.

James Watt's pastimes and tastes, indeed,
from earliest boyhood were very different from
those of other lads. His father kept a store
for the sale of articles used by ships, and it
was a favorite recreation of James to spend
his time there among the ropes, sails, and
tackle, finding out how they were made, and
to what uses they were devoted. He was
often found in the evening, too, sprawled at
full length on the sward of the hill near
Greenock, gazing for hours together at the
stars. Already an ambition to learn the
great secrets of astronomy had arisen in his
mind.

When he was fifteen years old, young Watt
was known in his neighborhood as a prodigy

of learning for his age.   He had now been to
school for a year or two, and had ardently
studied mathematics and natural philosophy.
At the same time he had learned a great deal
about mineralogy, chemistry, botany, and
physiology.   Not only had he derived much
knowledge from books, but he understood
how to apply this knowledge in many ways.
He had become a good carpenter; he knew
how to work in metals; and he took great
delight in making chemical experiments in a
little laboratory which he had fitted up at
home.   But perhaps the most wonderful thing
that he did was to construct a small electri-
cal machine, which astonished every one who
saw it.

There was a queer old man in Glasgow,
which was not very far from Greenock, who
kept a small dingy shop, where he mended
spectacles, fishing-tackle, and fiddles.   In this
shop young Watt worked for a while as an
apprentice.   But he was now eighteen years

old, and quite a man in his thoughts and aims.
He longed to make his way in the great
world; above all, he desired to see London,
and learn what could only be acquired in that
great city. So one day, supplied with a
small bundle of clothes, and accompanied by
his friend, John Marr, he set out for London
on horseback. It took the travellers ten days
to make their journey, and as Watt had
never before been far away from his native
place he saw many sights on the way which
interested and delighted him.

His father was poor, and Watt carried but
a small sum of money with him. So when
he at last reached London he looked up some
very humble lodgings in an obscure part of
the city. He ate only enough to keep body
and soul together, and after spending a few
days in viewing the wonders of the vast,
crowded capital, he set to work on his studies
with all his might. He took service with an
instrument-maker, and soon became very

skilful in making quadrants, compasses, and
other instruments.

But so delicate in health was he that he
soon broke down with hard work and meagre
fare, and was obliged to go back home again.
His native air restored his strength, and he
resumed work with redoubled zeal. At the
age of twenty-one Watt opened a shop of his
own in Glasgow, and put out his sign as a
mathematical-instrument maker. But he did
many other things besides making instruments. He constructed organs, fiddles, gui-
tars, and flutes. At the same time he pursued
other studies with the greatest ardor, and
soon knew a great deal about engineering,
natural history, languages, and literature. He
became well known to the professors and stu-
dents of Glasgow University, in the shade of
which his little shop stood, and his amiable
disposition and ripe knowledge made him a
great favorite with them, and secured him
many warm and valuable friends.

It was while Watt was engaged in these many busy and useful occupations that an incident occurred which changed the whole course of his life, and which in time led to fame and fortune. One day an old steam-engine, made by a man named Newcomen, was brought to him to repair. This engine was the best that had ever been invented; but it was a clumsy affair at best, and could not do better or quicker work than horses. As soon as Watt's keen eye examined it, he saw that the Newcomen engine was not good for much. Yet it showed him that an engine might be made which, with the use of steam, would perform wonders.

From that time he gave himself up to an absorbing study as to how to make a really useful and powerful steam-engine. There was something wanting — what was it? This was the question which perplexed him for days and weeks, and even years: how to keep the cylinder of the engine always as hot as the steam which entered it, and yet to have the cylinder get cold enough to condense the steam when the piston descended. Many a time Watt was on the point of giving up the problem in despair; but his resolute will kept him at work, and impelled him to persevere bravely.

One day, as with knitted brow he was sauntering across the Glasgow common, all of a sudden an idea struck him which solved the difficulty which had so long worried him. It occurred to him that, since steam was elastic, it would rush into any space or vessel the air in which had been exhausted. He hurried home in a fever of impatience. He constructed a vessel separate from the cylinder, and made a connection between them, and the vessel being exhausted of air, he found that the steam rushed into it.

This was the most important of all Watt's discoveries. He worked away on his engine now with redoubled zeal; but years were to

pass before his great object was fully achieved.
It was ten years after his walk on Glasgow
common before his idea had taken shape in
an actual working steam-engine. His health
more than once failed him, and on one occasion, so discouraged had he become, he bitterly
exclaimed, " Of all things in the world, there
is nothing so foolish as inventing ! "

But the triumph of his life, bringing with
it world-wide renown and ample wealth, came
at last.   About a hundred years ago Watt set
up his first complete steam-engine in London.
It saved labor, and in many industries at once
took the place of man and horse power.   All
the world saw after a while what a wonderful
machine it was; but no one then could have
foretold to what vast uses the idea of Watt's
engine was to be put.   We, who live in the
days of steamships, railways, great mills,
elevators, and a thousand other results of
Watt's invention, can more clearly see of what
enormous benefit it has been to mankind.

James Watt lived to a happy and prosperous old age, crowned with honors and revered by all his countrymen. He pursued his labors and researches to the end, and many were the ingenious devices which he invented. A fine statue of him stands in the Museum at Glasgow, near which the little model of his steam-engine, made by himself, was long kept for every one to see. The visitor to Westminster Abbey may observe among the memorials of poets, statesmen, and the most famous of Britain's sons, a statue of Watt, in a sitting posture, with an eloquent inscription by Lord Brougham. .

CHAPTER X

THE MONTGOLFIERS AND THE BALLOON

On a blustering winter's night in the latter part of the last century (1782), two brothers were seated before a blazing log fire near Lyons in France. The room in which they sat was situated in their paper manufactory, for their trade was the making of paper. Between the brothers, as they were comfortably toasting their knees at the fire, was a square table, and on the table a map was spread out. The two young men soon became absorbed in an earnest conversation. News had arrived that the giant fortress of Gibraltar, which had long been held by the English, was being vigorously besieged by the French fleet; and all Frenchmen were eagerly hoping for a victory by their countrymen. The Montgolfiers — this was the name of the brothers — were eagerly discussing the prospects of French success. Every now and then they would get up and bend over the map, and try to trace out the positions of the hostile forces at Gibraltar. At last, Stephen, the elder, pointing to a certain fortification on the map, exclaimed, " Ah, if our good fellows could only in some way get over *that*, victory would surely be theirs ! "

It happened that just then his wife came into the room with some clothes she had been washing. Spreading a line in front of the fire before which the brothers were sitting, she proceeded to hang up the clothes in order to dry them. Presently a petticoat fell off the line and floated over the blazing logs. Instead of falling into the fire, however, it became suddenly inflated, and, swelling out, it slowly floated up the chimney, out of sight.

The two brothers stared at the disappearing petticoat with wonder and amazement.

In a moment a startling idea flashed through Stephen's brain. What if a machine could be devised which would carry people through the air, by means of an inflated bag, just as this inflated petticoat had soared aloft? If such a device could be made, then the French soldiers might be carried safely over the obstructing rampart at Gibraltar, and the triumph would be won!

This is one version of the story of how the idea of the balloon first entered Stephen Montgolfier's head. Another version is that it was not the good dame's petticoat, but the paper cover of a conical sugar-loaf, which, being thrown upon the fire, became inflated and soared up the chimney.

Whichever story is the true one, it is certain that it was an accident which turned the thoughts of the Montgolfier brothers in the direction of making an air-machine which would enable people to travel in the air as well as on land and sea. But no accident

could have given such a hint to men of common intellect.   The Montgolfier brothers were
far above the ordinary French manufacturer
of their time in education and intelligence.
They were ardently fond of study, and while
they did not neglect their calling of paper-
making, they devoted their spare hours to
the reading of books, and to talking with
each other about what they had read.   Happily the two brothers had congenial tastes,
and were devotedly attached to each other.
When young they had not wasted their time
in pleasure-seeking, and from their entrance
upon active life their aims were high and
serious.

No sooner had the idea of air-machines
taken possession of their minds than they
became deeply absorbed in it.   Stephen, the
elder and more able of the two, devoted days
and nights to the construction of such a
machine.   At first he inflated a paper bag
with hydrogen, since hydrogen, being lighter

than air, would rise above it. But the gas escaped from the paper bag, and it thus became evident that paper was too light and frail a material for the purpose intended. The brothers next made a series of experiments with electricity, in the course of which they discovered that electricity lessened the weight of bodies. They made a rude balloon, and lit a fire under it, not only to rarefy the air, but also to supply a layer of electric fluid. This balloon was a large bag of silk, with a capacity of about forty cubic feet. As soon as it had been inflated by the fire applied beneath it, it rose rapidly until it bumped against the ceiling.

Stephen Montgolfier was now convinced that he had found a way to make a balloon, and he resolved to prove it publicly to the world. He accordingly announced that on a certain June day in 1783, a balloon would be inflated and sent aloft in the public square of Annonay, the town where he lived. When

Paris, and were speedily at work on another balloon. This time they resolved to use hydrogen instead of heated air for inflating their machine. The balloon was soon ready, and on a midsummer's day a tremendous crowd gathered on the Champ de Mars, in Paris, to see it ascend. Up it went when loosened from its moorings, floating high above the big city, and sweeping eastward, until it fell to the earth fifteen miles away.

Thus far, however, though the Montgolfiers had proved that a machine could be made which would travel in the air, no experiment had been made of carrying up human beings in it. At first the Montgolfiers thought they would try the effect of an aërial voyage on some of the lower animals. Accordingly, they attached a small car or basket to one of their balloons, and placed in it a duck, a sheep, and a cock. These first travellers of the air went aloft, and after remaining several thousand feet above the earth, came down all safe and sound. Then people began to think that in like manner men might trust themselves to the upper element. But at first it was thought safest to try a balloon which was fastened to the earth by ropes. In this way several men went up a hundred feet in a Montgolfier balloon. Then two men — the Marquis d'Arlandes and M. de Rozier — resolved that they would cut altogether loose from the earth, and risk the perils of a voyage in the upper air. Stephen Montgolfier set to work upon a balloon for this purpose. When it was finished he decorated it with ribbons and colors, and attached to its lower end a circular box or car for its human occupants.

Finally all was ready. The balloon was inflated at Passy, a suburb of Paris. A great multitude gathered to see the ascent of the first human beings who had ever mounted in the air far above the earth, while in Paris crowds occupied the towers of the cathedral of Notre Dame and other elevated points.

D'Arlandes and De Rozier took their places in the car, the word to cut loose was given, and up shot the balloon into the clouds which hung in the air. It ascended slowly and steadily to a height of three thousand feet, and then passed at an easy pace over the streets and houses of Paris. It completely crossed the city, and soon ascended to such a height that the occupants of the car could not see any of the objects on the earth below them. Then D'Arlandes became alarmed, and insisted on descending. As soon, therefore, as they had got clear of the city, so that they would not fall on the buildings, the air was suffered to gradually escape, and the balloon fell just outside Paris. More than a hundred years have passed since the memorable voyage of D'Arlandes and De Rozier in their Mont-golfier balloon ; but, although it is very common for men to make balloon voyages, no way has as yet been discovered for *guiding* balloons, and propelling them against the air-currents, and so making them practically useful for the purposes of travel.

CHAPTER XI

HUMPHRY DAVY AND THE SAFETY-LAMP

FEW boys have ever led a happier, busier, or more varied existence than did Humphry Davy. He was the son of a poor wood-carver, who lived in the pretty seaside town of Penzance, in England, where Humphry was born in 1778. Lowly, however, as was his birth, in his earliest years Humphry gave many proofs that nature had endowed him with rare talents.

Some of the stories told of his childish brightness are hard to believe. They relate, for instance, that before he was two years old he could talk almost as plainly and clearly as a grown person; that he could re-peat many passages of " Pilgrim's Progress," from having heard them, before he could read; and that at five years old he could read very rapidly, and remembered almost everything he read.

His father, the wood-carver, had died while Humphry was still very young, and had left his family poor. But by good-fortune a kind neighbor and friend, a Mr. Tonkine, took care of the widow and her children, and obtained a place for Humphry as an apprentice with an apothecary of the town. Humphry proved, indeed, a rather troublesome inmate of the apothecary's house. He set up a chemical laboratory in his little room upstairs, and there devoted himself to all sorts of experiments. Every now and then an explosion would be heard, which made the members of the apothecary's household quake with terror.

Humphry began to dream ambitious dreams. Not for him, he thought, was the drudgery of an apothecary store. He felt that he had in himself the making of a famous man, and he resolved that he would leave no science un-explored. He set to work with a will. His quick mind soon grasped the sciences not only of mathematics and chemistry, but of botany, anatomy, geology, and metaphysics. His means for the experiments he desired to make were very limited, but he did not allow any obstacle to prevent him from pursuing them.

He was especially fond of wandering along the seashore, and observing and examining the many curious and mysterious objects which he found on the crags and in the sand. One day his eye was struck with the bladders of seaweed, which he found full of air. The question was, how did the air get into them? This puzzled him, and he could find no answer to it, because he had no instruments to experiment with.

But on another day, soon after, as he strolled on the beach, what was his surprise and delight to find a case of surgical instru-ments, which had been flung up from some wreck on the coast! Armed with this, he hastened home, and managed to turn each one of the instruments to some useful account. He constructed an air-pump out of a surgeon's syringe, and made a great many experiments with it.

Fortunately for Humphry, he formed a friendship with a youth who could not only sympathize with him, but was of a great deal of use to him. This was Gregory Watt, a son of the great James Watt, the inventor of the steam-engine. Gregory Watt had gone to Penzance for his health, and had there fallen in with the ambitious son of the wood-carver. This new friend was able to give Humphry many new and valuable hints, and encouraged him with hopeful words to go on with his studies and experiments.

Already Humphry was getting to be known as a scientific genius beyond the quiet neighborhood of Penzance. He had proposed a theory on heat and light which had attracted

the attention of learned men; and at twenty-
one he had discovered the peculiar properties
of nitrous oxide — what we now call "laugh-
ing-gas" — though he nearly killed himself
by inhaling too much of it. He had also
made many experiments in galvanism, and
had found silicious earth in the skin of reeds
and grass.

So famous indeed had he already become,
that at the age of twenty-two — when most
young men are only just leaving college — he
was chosen lecturer on science at the great
Royal Institution in London. There he
amazed men by the eloquence and clearness
with which he revealed the mysteries of
science. He was so bright and attractive a
young man, moreover, that the best London
society gladly welcomed him to its drawing-
rooms, and praises of him were in every
mouth. His lecture-room was crowded whenever he spoke.

But he was not a bit spoiled by all this

flattery and homage. He worked all the harder; resolved to achieve yet greater triumphs in science than he had yet done. An opportunity soon arose to turn his knowledge and inventive powers to account in a very important way. For a long time the English public had every now and then been horrified by the terrible explosions which took place in the coál mines. These explosions resulted often in an appalling loss of human life. Their cause was the filling of the mine by a deadly gas, called "fire-damp," which, when ignited by a lighted candle or lamp, exploded with fearful violence. One day an explosion of fire-damp occurred which killed over one hundred miners on the spot.

This event called universal attention to the subject, and Humphry Davy was besought to try and find some means of preventing, or at least lessening, similar calamities. He promptly undertook the task, and set about it with all his wonted energy. The problem before him was how to provide light in the mines in such a way that the miners might see to work by it, and at the same time be safe from the danger of fire-damp explosion. Many attempts had been made to achieve this, but they had all failed.

Davy began his experiments. He soon made several valuable discoveries. One was that explosions of inflammable gases could not pass through long narrow metallic tubes. Another was that when he held a piece of wire gauze over a lighted candle, the flame would not pass through it. As a result of his long and patient toil Davy was able at last to construct his now famous *Safety-Lamp*, which has undoubtedly saved the lives of thousands during the period which has elapsed since it was invented. He presented a model of his new lamp to the Royal Society, in whose rooms in London it is to be seen to this day.

It is a simple affair, being merely a lamp screwed on to a wire gauze cylinder, and fitted to it by a tight ring. His idea was to admit the fire-damp into the lamp gradually by narrow tubes, so that it would be consumed by combustion. The Safety-Lamp was in truth the greatest triumph of Humphry Davy's useful life.

" I value it," he said, " more than anything I ever did."

Honors of all kinds were showered upon him. Many medals were awarded to him, and the grateful miners subscribed from their scant wages enough to present him with a magnificent service of silver worth $12,000. His discovery was hailed from every part of Europe. The Czar Alexander of Russia sent him a beautiful vase, and he was chosen a member of the historic Institute of France; while his own government conferred upon him the coveted title of baronet.

Sir Humphry Davy, as he was now called, died in the prime of life and in the fulness of honor and fame. Fond of travel, and continuing to the last his scientific studies, he went to the Continent, and took up his abode at Geneva, on the borders of one of the loveliest of Swiss lakes. There he had a laboratory, where he could work at will, and could also indulge his passion for fishing and hunting.

But he was worn out before his time. He was attacked by palsy, and passed away at Geneva in 1829, in the fifty-first year of his age. There he was buried. A simple monument reveals where he lies in the foreign churchyard; while a tablet in Westminster Abbey keeps alive his memory in the hearts of his countrymen.

CHAPTER XII

JAMES NASMYTH AND THE STEAM-HAMMER

THE roll of modern inventors contains no more attractive name than that of the sturdy Scot who invented the marvellous steam-hammer. The life of James Nasmyth was a romance. His achievements were noble, his success was brilliant, and his character was so cheerful, sunny, upright, and happy, that it is a delight to dwell upon it.

He himself has told us, in words of simple, hearty enthusiasm, the story of his boyhood and of the triumphs of his manhood. It is curious that his very name had a history in striking contrast with the actual facts of his life. One of his ancestors, it is said, in trying to escape from the enemy on a battle-field, assumed the disguise of a blacksmith. He was caught, after a sharp race, when his captor, perceiving his disguise, exclaimed, —

"Why, ye are *nae* smyth" (no smith); whence came the family name of Nasmyth.

Now no greater *smith* ever lived than this James of the contrary name, who made the steam-hammer. The old warlike family motto too, "Non arte, sed marte" (Not by art, but by war), was so entirely contrary to James Nasmyth's pursuits that he turned it entirely around, and made it, " Non marte, sed arte" (Not by war, but by art). It was, indeed, by his masterful art that he achieved triumphs more enduring for the good of mankind than any war has ever done. Let us see what an unusual kind of a boy James Nasmyth was.

He came of a very practical and mechanical family. His grandfather was an architect of Edinburgh, while his father was not only a very fair artist in colors, but was also skilful as an architect and as a mechanic. James was born and brought up in the quaint old Scottish capital. His mother was a shrewd, keen-witted Scotchwoman, who very early in her boy's life perceived that he was a " very noticin' bairn." When James, in his teens, was at the Edinburgh High School, his mechanical ingenuity quickly became apparent.

The favorite toys of the Edinburgh boys at that time were spinning-tops and small cannon. James thought he could make better tops and cannon than they sold at the stores. So he set to work with his father's foot-lathe, and soon made tops which delighted his school comrades beyond measure. He also made little brass cannon which worked perfectly, and even out of old keys contrived to fashion a small hand-gun. Flying kites and paper balloons he easily constructed, and he made himself wondrously popular at school by freely supplying his mates with these means of enjoying their holidays.

He soon became deeply interested in chemistry. The father of one of his schoolmates had a chemical laboratory at Leith, a mile or so distant from Edinburgh, and to this laboratory young Nasmyth was freely admitted. When some interesting experiment was about to be made, Tom Smith, Nasmyth's young friend, would hoist a white flag on a pole in the garden at Leith, whereat Nasmyth eagerly ran down and took part in the experiment. The boys not only had a hand in the experiments, but taught themselves how to make each material used in them, instead of buying them in the stores. Thus Nasmyth soon became a very skilful practical chemist.

At the age of seventeen young Nasmyth began to turn his mechanical talents to practical account. He made a little steam-engine for grinding his father's colors; he constructed some workshop engines, and the model of a condensing engine to be used at mechanics' institutes; and after attending for four or five years the Edinburgh School of Arts, made the model of a steam-carriage for railway purposes. For it was just at that time, when Nasmyth was nineteen, that the possibility of applying steam to land travel was on the point of being proved.

It took Nasmyth four months of absorbing labor to complete his steam-carriage, and when done it was run successfully on the Queensberry Road, near Edinburgh, carrying eight passengers, who sat upon low seats only three feet from the ground. This seems to us now a very rude and uncouth way of travelling, but when Nasmyth's steam-carriage proved to be a success, it was looked upon as a wonder of wonders.

One of the most important events of young Nasmyth's life was when he was admitted to the famous works of Henry Maudsley in London. Mr. Maudsley was an eccentric but kind-hearted man, and very able in mechanical work, and his reputation was world-wide. He had long refused to admit any more pupils in his works; but he was so struck with the genius shown in the models which Nasmyth displayed to him, that he not only accepted the young Scot as a pupil, but took him into his own private workshop.

"Here I wish you to work," said Maudsley, "beside me, as my assistant."

Nasmyth remained with this generous patron two years, when Maudsley died.

Nasmyth was now fully equipped for his life-work. He took charge of a large foundry near Manchester, where he soon acquired more than a competence.

He was one of those who had the rare privilege of witnessing the opening of the first railway, — that between Manchester and Liverpool — and to see Stephenson's "Rocket" draw the first train out of Manchester. The establishment of railways gave abundance of work to Nasmyth, who now made locomotives for the new companies which rapidly sprang up.

But the great achievement of Nasmyth's life was the invention of that powerful *steam-hammer*, which still continues to be a marvel to all who see its operation, at once mighty and delicate. It is said of this machine that it can chip an egg resting on an anvil without breaking it, while it can also deliver a twelve-ton blow which will make a whole township tremble. We cannot do better than quote Nasmyth's own description of this crowning mechanical triumph of his life.

"It consisted of, first, a massive anvil on which to rest the work; second, a block of iron constituting the hammer or blow-giving portion; and third, an inverted steam-cylinder, to whose piston-rod the hammer-block was attached. All that was then required to produce a most effective hammer was simply

to admit steam of sufficient pressure into the cylinder so as to act on the under side of the piston, and thus to raise the hammer block attached to the end of the piston-rod.

" By a very simple arrangement of a slide valve, under the control of an attendant, the steam was allowed to escape, and thus permit the massive block of iron rapidly to descend by its own gravity upon the work then on the anvil. Thus, by the more or less rapid manner in which the attendant allows the steam to enter or escape from the cylinder, any required number or any intensity of blows can be delivered."

One of the first uses to which the steam-hammer was put was that of the driving of piles. There were many mechanics who did not believe that it would drive piles faster or better than was done by the old method. So Nasmyth resolved to have a match between his steam-hammer and the ordinary pile-driver. Two immense logs were selected, and the two machines began to work at the same moment. The result was that while it took the old-fashioned machine twelve hours to drive its log to the proper depth, the steam-hammer had finished its task in four and a half minutes.

The invention of the steam-hammer not only made Nasmyth famous wherever in the world the mechanic arts are practised, but added quickly and largely to his worldly wealth. He was only thirty-one years of age, and had already achieved a great life-work.

CHAPTER XIII

GEORGE STEPHENSON, THE INVENTOR OF THE RAILWAY LOCOMOTIVE

IN the north of England, in a district through which flows the river Tyne, and of which the principal town is Newcastle, there is a vast region of coal-mines. For a long period this region has been a busy scene of grimy labor, with its clusters of villages inhabited by the coal-miners, its railways running from the mouths of the coal-pits to the river-bank, and its appliances for raising the coal from the dark depths of the nether earth.

One of the villages, occupied for the most part by miners, is called Dewley Burn. It is but a short distance from Newcastle, the smoking chimneys of which may be plainly descried from its cottage windows. It was at Dewley Burn that there lived, just about a hundred years ago, a very remarkable little boy — a boy whose father was nothing but a humble colliery fireman, and very poor at that ; a boy who had never seen the inside of a schoolhouse in his life; yet who, even before he had reached his teens, showed unmistakable signs of brilliant genius, and who in after-life was destined to become one of the most famous men in the history of the world.

George Stephenson — this was the boy's name — was forced to learn the stern realities of a life of labor at a very early age. His father had six children, and his wages were only three dollars a week. Each of his boys, therefore, had to go to work just as soon as he was old enough to turn his hands to anything at all. So we find George, when he was but seven years old, sent off to the fields to tend a herd of cows. The little fellow

was bare-headed and bare-legged ; his clothes
scarcely sufficed to cover his active little body.
But he was quick, bright, and light-hearted,
and always went whistling or singing merrily
to his daily task.

Even at that early age George Stephenson's
fondness for mechanics, which in after-years
was destined to confer a vast benefit upon the
whole human race, revealed itself.   When he
had an hour or two to spare he did not spend
it in idleness or in playing games or strolling about with his mates. Instead, he always
hastened to the engine-room where his father
was at work.   He delighted in nothing so
much as to watch the movements of the
engine, and to study the different parts of it,
and the use of each.   The engine seemed to
his keen mind the most curious and wonderful thing in the world.   He was never tired
of gazing at it as its every part moved swiftly
and smoothly up and down or to and fro.

One day George was in the field just outside

the village tending his herd as usual. While, however, he kept his eye from time to time on the cows, he was observed by a villager to be busily working at something with his hands. The villager went up to him, and found that he had moulded a little engine out of clay, and had inserted in his model pipes made of hemlock stalks. This was the first engine George Stephenson ever built. The last that he built, many years after, revolutionized the whole trade, commerce, and comfort of the earth.

George Stephenson all through his boyhood and youth had a hard life of it, though it never was an unhappy one. Early accustomed to hardship and rugged tasks, he worked always blithely, and, indeed, seems really to have loved his work. While other boys of his age were going to school, he was tending cows, ploughing, hoeing potatoes and turnips, and finally aiding his father as assistant fireman on wages of twenty-five cents a day. When he was fifteen he was made very proud by being promoted to be a full-blown fireman to an engine, on wages of three dollars a week. "Now," exclaimed the delighted youth, when he told his father of his promotion, " I am a made man for life ! "

So the hard-working years passed until George reached his eighteenth birthday. Up to this time, strange to say, he had not had an hour's schooling. It is odd to think that at eighteen George Stephenson, who a few years after was recognized as one of the greatest men of science the world ever produced, could neither read, write, nor cipher ! Yet he was intelligent, keen, and ambitious. He was a complete master of the engine, and his brain was already teeming with bright ideas and with devices for improving the machinery then in use. He saw clearly how much in need he was of some education, and he resolved that, hard as he had to work at his trade by day, he would begin to learn something from books. So, when his long task of twelve hours was done, he ate a hasty supper, and repaired three evenings every week to school. In less than a year he had learned to read and write, and had mastered his arithmetic from cover to cover.

The next phase of young Stephenson's life is a pretty love story. He had now been promoted to be the brakeman of a large coalmine, and his wages were about five dollars a week. Not content with this, he employed his leisure evenings in mending shoes. It so happened that he had made the acquaintance of a pretty maid, who lived at a farm a mile or two away from the village. Her name was Fanny Henderson. Soon Stephenson found himself very much in love with her. One day Fanny asked him if he would not mend her shoes for her. He accepted the task with eager delight. He was so fond of the pretty owner of the shoes, that after he had mended them, he could not bear to carry

them back to her at once, but kept them in
his pocket for some days as he went to his
work. Every now and then he would take
them out and gaze fondly at them, and returned them at last with a sigh of regret.

His love for the fair Fanny stirred him to
work all the harder, and by the time he was
twenty-one he had saved up enough money to
hire and furnish a cottage. Then one morning he took Fanny to church, where they
were quietly married. After the knot was
tied they both got upon the same horse and
so rode blithely home to the newly furnished
cottage. The married life of young Stephenson and his Fanny was very happy, but very
brief. In a few years the young wife died,
leaving an only son. This son, Robert, was
destined, in after years, to rival his father in
renown as an inventor and engineer.

George Stephenson, though grief-stricken
by his great loss, continued to work with all
his wonted, untiring vigor. In order to give

little Robert the education of which he himself so sorely felt the need, he added to his labor as a brakeman the cleaning of his neighbors' clocks and watches. "It was thus," he said afterward, "that I procured the means of educating my little son."

The time was fast coming, however, when Stephenson, by his genius and energy, was to raise himself forever above the pains and troubles of poverty. It came about in this way. As a boy he had often seen the tramway of parallel rails, upon which the car-loads of coal had been drawn by horses from the mines to the banks of the Tyne. A few years later, as we have seen, he had learned all about steam-engines, and had mastered the structure and powers of the perfected steam-engine invented by James Watt. The brilliant thought now occurred to Stephenson that the engine might be so adapted as to work upon parallel rails, and might be so made as to take the place of horses in dragging car-loads.   Hitherto the steam-engine had been used as a stationary machine.   He proposed to make it move and travel.   He set himself the task, as he said, of "wedding the engine to the rail, as man to wife."

It is not easy to imagine what an enormous task this was ; what great and various difficulties he had to meet and overcome ; what violent opposition and prejudices he had to baffle and conquer.   It was years before Stephenson was able to construct a steam-locomotive which would actually go on rails. When he had succeeded in this, he had yet to persuade an unbelieving community that he could successfully draw trains of cars with it over the parallel rails.

The first successful trip made by his steam-locomotive was made on a little tramway at Kittingworth.   It drew a train of cars with a load of thirty tons, up a steep grade, at the rate of four miles an hour.   This proved to Stephenson that, beyond a doubt, the locomotive might be used for hauling not only freight, but passengers also.   At last, a little less than sixty years ago, the first regular railway line was completed between Manchester and Liverpool.   Upon the new track was placed a small train of passenger cars, with Stephenson's new locomotive, the "Rocket," puffing in front of it.   Railways had become an actual fact, and Stephenson's victory was complete.

CHAPTER XIV

ROBERT STEPHENSON, THE GREAT BRIDGE-BUILDER

IT will be remembered that while George
Stephenson, the noble-hearted inventor of the
railway locomotive, was still struggling for a
livelihood, he lost his young wife, who left
behind an only infant son. A famous father
is seldom followed by a son equally famous.
But the little boy who was thus left mother-
less became in course of time not less cele-
brated than George Stephenson himself. The
two names stand side by side in the bright
roll of the benefactors of their age; just as
they two worked side by side for many years,
together laboring upon and finally solving
the problem of the locomotive, and winning
many other brilliant scientific triumphs.

The story of Robert Stephenson, indeed, is

not less interesting and inspiring than that of his father. Left without a mother's tender care, the boy at a very early age became his father's intimate companion, and was the joy and pride of his father's life. From the first he revealed a quick, bright mind, and, to his father's great delight, showed a taste for study, and especially for mechanics. George Stephenson had not yet become rich or famous. He was still plodding with cheerful industry, at his shoe-making and clock-making, varying these occupations with reading scientific books and constructing models. He had learned by his own experience what an obstacle ignorance of books was to getting on fast in the world; and so, just as soon as Robert was old enough to go to school, to school he was sent.

But this was not all the early education he had. At Newcastle, a short distance from their home, there was a library for working people, to which George Stephenson secured

admittance for his son.   Out of school hours,
then, you might have seen little Robert trudg-
ing on the road to the big town, repairing to
the library, reading for an hour or two, and
then returning home again.   In the winter
evenings he would sit down at the cosey coal
fire opposite his father, and would carefully
repeat to him what he had been reading at
the library.   So the boy in a way taught his
hard-working father, while impressing upon
his own mind the results of his reading.   Not
only did they study together, they also made
models and plans for machinery together.
Robert proved to be amazingly quick and apt
in this practical work.   Once he made a very
accurate sun-dial, which his father delightedly
fixed on the wall over the door of his little
cottage.

When Robert was fifteen he went to work
in the same colliery where his father was now
employed as engineer.   After the day's work
was over, every evening was spent by the two

in study, or in discussing useful subjects with each other. They often held very exciting arguments as to the power of steam, and as to the possibility of applying it to locomotion. Already in both minds the locomotive was beginning to take form and shape. Little by little George Stephenson carefully hoarded his savings, until he had enough to send Robert to Edinburgh, to the university there. It is true that the young man only remained at the university six months; but during that brief time he is said to have done as much studying as most college boys do in three years. Proud indeed was his father when Robert returned from Edinburgh with the prize for mathematics. It is said that Robert learned how to write shorthand before going to Edinburgh, and that while at the university he took down every lecture that he heard, word for word.

George Stephenson had now matured his plan for a railway locomotive, and had established a factory for building locomotives at Newcastle. Robert now joined him, and for two years worked hard to make the machine a practicable one. Then his health broke down from overwork, and he took a long voyage to South America. But he did not spend his time while away in idleness and pleasure-seeking. Ever earnest of purpose, and intensely interested in the products and forces of the world, he visited the gold and silver mines, founded a mining company, and planned the machinery for it.

After an absence of three years, he returned to England to find his father preparing to make the great experiment of running a locomotive by steam. He threw himself with all the energy of his nature into the project, and did more perhaps than even his father to perfect the first successful locomotive, the "Rocket." This engine received the prize of five hundred pounds offered by the new Liverpool and Manchester Railway Company. It may well be supposed that Robert exulted as greatly as his father when at last the little "Rocket" sped safely with its first train from Manchester to Liverpool.

But though the world is probably indebted as much to Robert as to George Stephenson for the inestimable gift of steam locomotion by land, the son won yet greater renown by his later triumphs as an engineer. For some years he devoted himself to laying out and building railway lines in his own country, Belgium, Norway, Switzerland, Germany, Canada, Egypt, and India. Honors and wealth were showered upon him by the grateful nations which he thus served. By the time he had reached middle age he might have retired to a life of ease and enjoyment. But Robert Stephenson loved work; idleness would have been torture to his vigorous and untiring brain.

He now turned with youthful energy to the construction of great bridges, and in this pursuit he achieved many very remarkable triumphs. Those of our readers who have travelled in Canada, and have visited Montreal, cannot have failed to gaze with wonder at the mighty Victoria Bridge, which spans the St. Lawrence near that historic city. This noble structure, with the graded roadways leading to it on either bank, covers a space of but little short of two miles. It has been well said that " in its gigantic strength and majestic proportions there is no structure to compare with it in ancient or modern times." It consists of a series of twenty-five great tubular bridges, with a vast central span springing more than three hundred feet. The iron-work which the bridge easily uplifts in the air weighs no less than ten thousand tons, and the piers comprise stone-work each of eight thousand tons weight. It may be safely declared that this Victoria Bridge, designed and built by the bold genius of Robert Stephenson, dwarfs all the mightiest works of Roman engineering.

Two other bridges of world-wide fame were built by Stephenson. One is the Highland Bridge, which spans the river Tyne at Newcastle very near where both George and Robert Stephenson were born; and the other, yet more wonderful, is the Britannia Bridge, which at Menai Straits, on the Welsh coast, leaps high across a broad inlet of the ocean, at such an elevation that " vessels of large burden in full sail can pass beneath its lofty arches."

All these bridges were built on what is called the " tubular " principle — an idea invented by Robert Stephenson himself. The main structure of the tubular bridge comprises a tunnel of wrought-iron, within which the railway trains pass to and fro. The Britannia Bridge has four of these tunnels or tubes, each two hundred and sixty feet long. Besides these bridges, Stephenson built one over the Damietta branch of the Nile in Egypt, and another at Bekat-al-Saba, in the same country.

Even such vast labors did not exhaust Robert Stephenson's energies. While supervising the building of his bridges he had time to study various systems of water-works, to help Sir Joseph Paxton in his designs for the great first World's Exhibition in Hyde Park, and to take his seat in Parliament, where his scientific knowledge enabled him to be especially useful. He was also a member of many learned and scientific societies, in all of which he took an active part. Nor amid all his fame did he forget the humble place of his birth. He took down the cottage in which he was born, and caused buildings to be erected on the spot where it had stood, which were used as a school for poor boys and girls, and for a mechanics' institute.

This great and good man died at the early age of fifty-six, and was laid to rest in Westminster Abbey, among famous kings, nobles, poets, and philosophers.

CHAPTER XV

ROBERT FULTON AND THE STEAMBOAT

THERE are few more interesting or dramatic stories in the history of science than that which relates to the invention of steamboats. This story, curiously enough, reaches far back into the remote past and among ancient peoples. The paddle-wheel, for instance, by which steamboats are propelled even down to our own day, is said to have been known to the ancient Egyptians, and to have been used by them on the river Nile. The Chinese were probably acquainted with it as far back at least as the seventh century. Twenty years before Columbus crossed the Atlantic on his voyage of discovery, pictures of paddle-wheels for the moving of vessels were to be seen in Europe. Roger Bacon,

seven hundred years ago, mentioned this device as one well suited to the navigating of
rivers.

In the seventeenth century dim hints were
given that other agencies than the human
muscle might be used as the power for the
moving of small vessels. Denis Papin, the
famous French inventor, for instance, proposed that the oars of boats should be moved
by heat. Savery shortly after declared his
belief that the rude little steam-engine which
he had invented might be used to propel
paddle-wheels. In 1724 John Dickens asserted that a vessel could be driven against
wind and tide by forcing water through its
stern and by firing gunpowder to move the
engines. James Watt invented several devices which led almost directly to the idea of
the steamboat. The Marquis de Jouffroy in
France, Fitch and Rumsey in America, and
Miller and Symington in Scotland, clearly
perceived that it was possible to apply steam

to lake and river navigation, long before the steamboat was finally perfected.

The very first steamboat which actually puffed its way over the water was built by James Symington, and was launched on a bleak autumn morning in 1788 on the Scottish lake of Dalswinton. On board the little craft, as it sped over the waves at the then astounding rate of five miles an hour, were a number of famous men. There were Alexander Nasmyth, a famous artist, the father of James Nasmyth who invented the steamhammer; Henry Brougham, afterward Lord High Chancellor of England; and Robert Burns, soon to be known through the world as a great poet. But, curiously enough, though Symington's steamboat proved that steam could be used to propel vessels, the idea was not then adopted and followed up. After several more trials Symington's device fell into disuse. Its immense importance was not perceived.

It was the task of Robert Fulton, an
American, to establish for all time the fact
that steam navigation could be made practical and permanent. Robert Fulton was a
native of Pennsylvania, and in early life revealed a marked talent as an artist. He
took lessons in painting, and for many years
pursued his art with ardor. His parents
were poor, yet Fulton managed to procure
enough money to go to Europe, where at
twenty-one we find him studying under the
great court painter, Benjamin West. Himself an American, West found a pride in
guiding his bright-eyed young countryman in
his efforts to become a good artist. But
while in England, Fulton seems to have been
diverted from art in order to study mechanics.
He soon showed that his genius lay in the
direction of inventing. At first he aided the
Duke of Bridgewater in the construction of
the canal known by that nobleman's name,
inventing inclined planes for locks for the

passage of canal-boats. Then he invented a mill for the sawing of marble, and new methods of making ropes.

It was at this time that the experiments of Symington and others in applying steam to navigation were creating a great deal of attention in England, and Fulton soon became absorbed in this new problem. He was a young man of sensitive and enthusiastic nature, somewhat frail in health, but endowed with a keen, quick intellect and a courageous, persistent spirit. He made up his mind that he himself would establish finally and forever the possibility of navigation by steam. Fulton was an ardent lover of his native land as well as an inventive genius. As he thought with glowing pride of the fifty thousand miles of navigable rivers which flowed through our Western States, inviting to them population, capital, and business energy, he saw that the steamboat, if it could be perfected, would be the means of developing those vast, rich, and fertile Western lands.

So he set to work with a will, and devoted himself exclusively to the problem of steam navigation for fourteen years. At the age of thirty-one he repaired to Paris. His fame as an engineer was already great, and Edward Livingston, then the American Minister to France, and a very enlightened, liberal, and public-spirited man, invited him to become an inmate of his house. Fulton lived for some years under Mr. Livingston's hospitable roof, all the time working at his task with all his might. He overcame many obstacles, and rose with renewed energy from many failures. He sought the advice of the great inventors of the day, such as Watt and Cartwright, who gladly lent their aid to the bright young toiler. He made many experiments, and on one occasion a steamboat which he had built was launched on the river Seine. This, however, did not work well.

A less resolute spirit than Fulton's might have despaired ; but he kept straight on, undaunted by his want of success. When in process of time his project came to the notice of the great Napoleon, that famous man declared that " it was capable of changing the face of the entire world."

At last Fulton became satisfied that he could build and launch a successful steamboat. His good and generous friend, Mr. Livingston, had not lost faith in him, and shared his confidence. Mr. Livingston gave Fulton a large sum of money with which to build a steamboat on his latest plan, and Fulton sailed for New York. There he at once set about carrying out his scheme. This time the steamboat which he constructed seemed to him to fulfil every condition of success.

This steamboat he named the " Clermont." It was on a morning in August, 1807, that the " Clermont," all completed, with her engine

The Clermont Steaming Up the Hudson.   Page 166.

duly equipped and fixed, — a novel sight for the lookers-on to see, — lay moored at her dock in the North River. The momentous day for her first trip had arrived. A crowd assembled at the dock to see her start. Fulton, with beating heart, stood on the little deck, surrounded by a group of curious and anxious friends. The word was given, the engine was started, and the " Clermont " pushed out upon the stream. Then, after going a little way, the boat suddenly stopped. It was a moment of harrowing suspense to the brave inventor. A slight hitch in the machinery was speedily discovered. It was quickly set right, and the " Clermont," amid murmurs of wonder and delight, resumed her voyage.

As she steamed up the Hudson, by the Palisades, between the lofty banks of Yonkers and Tarrytown, past the wooded heights of West Point, the country people from miles around gathered on the shore on either side to witness her progress. They were bewildered and terrified. The "Clermont," indeed, seemed to their eyes "a monster moving on the water, defying the winds and tide, and breathing flames and smoke." When the crews of the river boats heard the rumble of her machinery and the splashing of her paddles, and saw the steam and sparks bursting from her valves and funnel, they flew below-deck in their fright; or, prostrating themselves on deck, prayed to be protected from "the horrible creature which was marching on the tides and lighting its path by the fires which it vomited."

The "Clermont," however, reached Albany in safety, and Fulton and his friends stepped exultantly on shore. His great end, after so many years of difficulty, trial, and perseverance, was at last accomplished. Steam navigation had become a fact. The great test had been successful; and thenceforth all the waters of the earth were to swarm with steam-vessels, of which the little "Clermont" was the parent and the pioneer.

After this, Fulton built other steamboats, one of which was a steam-frigate. But, as is the case with most great inventors, no sooner was he successful than dishonest men attempted to reap for themselves the reward of his long labors. His patents were disputed, and he was involved in a long series of weary lawsuits. Deeply suffering under these vexations, his sensitive nature and frailty of constitution brought him to the grave, and he died in 1815, at the age of forty-nine. Fulton was known as a man of social feelings and generous nature, and his death called forth general mourning throughout the land of which he had always been so proud, and which honored him as one of the foremost inventors and benefactors of the time.

CHAPTER XVI

THE STRUGGLES OF CHARLES GOODYEAR

NEVER did any man work harder, suffer more keenly, or remain more steadfast to one great purpose of life, than did Charles Goodyear. The story of his life — for the most part mournful — teems with touching interest. No inventor ever struggled against greater or more often returning obstacles, or against repeated failures more overwhelming. Goodyear is often compared, as a martyr and hero of invention, to Bernard Palissy the potter. He is sometimes called "the Palissy of the nineteenth century." But his sufferings were more various, more bitter, and more long enduring than ever were even those of Palissy; while the result of his long, unceasing labors was infinitely more precious to the world. For if Palissy restored the art of enamelling so as to produce beautiful works of art, Goodyear perfected a substance which gives comfort and secures health to millions of human beings.

Charles Goodyear was born at New Haven, Connecticut, in the first year of the present century. He was the eldest of the six children of a leading hardware merchant of that place, a man both of piety and of inventive talent. When Charles was a boy, his father began the manufacture of hardware articles, and at the same time carried on a farm. He often required his son's assistance, so that Charles's schooling was limited. He was very fond of books, however, from an early age, and instead of playing with his mates, devoted most of his leisure time to reading.

It was even while he was a schoolboy that his attention was first turned to the material, the improvement of which for common uses became afterwards his life-work. "He happened to take up a thin scale of India-rubber," says his biographer, "peeled from a bottle, and it was suggested to his mind that it would be a very useful fabric if it could be made uniformly so thin, and could be so prepared as to prevent its melting and sticking together in a solid mass." Often afterward he had a vivid presentiment that he was destined by Providence to achieve these results.

The years of his youth and early manhood were spent in the hardware trade in Philadelphia and then in Connecticut; and at twenty-four he was married to a heroic young wife, who shared his trials, and was ever to him a comforting and encouraging spirit. From boyhood he was always devout and pure in habits. On one occasion, soon after his marriage, he wrote to his wife while absent from her: "I have quit smoking, chewing, and drinking all in one day. You cannot form an idea of the extent of this last evil in this city [New York] among the young men."

Charles Goodyear's misfortunes began early in his career. He failed in business, his health broke down, and through life thereafter he suffered from almost continual attacks of dyspepsia. He was, moreover, a small, frail man, with a weak constitution. He was imprisoned for debt after his failure; nor was this the only time that he found himself within the walls of a jail. That was almost a frequent experience with him in after life.

It was under discouragements like these that Goodyear began his long series of experiments in India-rubber. Already this peculiar substance — a gum that exudes from a certain kind of very tall tree, which is chiefly found in South America — had been manufactured into various articles, but it had not been made enduring, and the uses to which it could be put were very limited.

There is no space here to follow Goodyear's experiments in detail. He entered upon them with the ardor of a fanatic and the faith of a devotee. But he very soon found that the difficulties in his way were great and many. He was bankrupt, in bad health, with a growing family dependent on him, and no means of support. Yet he persevered, through years of wretchedness, to the very end. It is a striking fact that his very first experiment was made in a prison cell.

During the long period occupied by his repeated trials of invention he passed through almost every calamity to which human flesh is heir. Again and again he was thrown into prison. Repeatedly he saw starvation staring him and his gentle wife and his poor little children in the face. He was reduced many times to the very last extreme of penury. His friends sneered at him, deserted him, called him mad. He was forced many times to beg the loan of a few dollars, with no prospect of repayment.   One of his children died in the dead of winter, when there was no fuel in the cheerless house.   A gentleman was once asked what sort of a looking man Goodyear was.   "If you meet a man," was the reply, "who wears an India-rubber coat, cap, stock, vest, and shoes, with an India-rubber money purse without a cent in it, that is Charles Goodyear."

Once, while in the extremity of want, when he was living at Greenwich, near New York, he met his brother-in-law, and said, "Give me ten dollars, brother; I have pawned my last silver spoon to pay my fare to the city."

"You must not go on so; you cannot live in this way," said the other.

"I am going to do better," replied Goodyear cheerily.

It was by accident at last that he hit upon the secret of how to make India-rubber durable.   He was talking one day to several

visitors, and in his ardor making rapid gest-
ures, when a piece of rubber which he was
holding in his hand accidentally hit against a
hot stove. To his amazement, instead of
melting, the gum remained stiff and charred,
like leather. He again applied great heat to
a piece of rubber, and then nailed it outside
the door, where it was very cold. The next
morning he found that it was perfectly flexible; and this was the discovery which led to
that successful invention which he had struggled through so many years to perfect. The
main value of the discovery lay in this, that
while the gum would dissolve in a moderate
heat, it both remained hard and continued to
be flexible when submitted to an extreme
heat. This came to be known as the "vul-
canization" of India-rubber.

Two years were still to elapse, however,
before Goodyear could make practical use of
his great discovery. He had tired everybody out by his previous frequent assertions

that his invention had been perfected, when it had until now always proved a failure. Many a time he had gone to his friends, declaring that he had succeeded, so that when he really had made the discovery nobody believed in it.

He was still desperately poor and in wretched health. Yet he moved to Woburn, in Massachusetts, resolutely continuing his experiments there. He had no money, and so baked his India-rubber in his wife's oven and saucepans, or hung it before the nose of her tea-kettle. Sometimes he begged the use of the factory ovens in the neighborhood after the day's work was over, and sold his children's very school-books in order to supply himself with the necessary gum. At this time he lived almost exclusively on money gifts from pitying friends, who shook their heads in their doubts of his sanity. Often his house had neither food nor fuel in it; his family were forced to go out into the woods to get wood to burn. "They dug their potatoes before they were half-grown, for the sake of having something to eat."

Goodyear was terribly afraid that he should die before he could make the world perceive the great uses to which his discovery might be applied. What he was toiling for was neither fame nor fortune, but only to confer a vast benefit on his fellow-men.

At last, after infinite struggles, the absorbing purpose of his life was attained. India-rubber was introduced under his patents, and soon proved to have all the value he had, in his wildest moments, claimed for it. Success thus crowned his noble efforts, which had continued unceasingly through ten years of self-imposed privation. India-rubber was now seen to be capable of being adapted to at least five hundred uses. It could be made " as pliable as kid, tougher than ox-hide, as elastic as whale-bone, or as rigid as flint." But, as too often happens, his great discovery enriched neither

Goodyear nor his family. It soon gave employment to sixty thousand artisans, and annually produced articles in this country alone worth eight millions of dollars.

Happily the later years of the noble, self-devoted inventor were spent at least free from the grinding penury and privations of his years of uncertainty and toil. He died in his sixtieth year (1860), happy in the thought of the magnificent boon he had given to mankind.

CHAPTER XVII

ELIAS HOWE AND THE SEWING-MACHINE

IN the enlightened days of the nineteenth century the great inventors enjoy a brighter and sunnier lot than did those who lived in ruder and darker times. The modern inventor is seldom the victim of ignorance. He is no longer hunted down by fierce and fanatical superstition. He is no longer thought to be a sorcerer; for his magic is seen to be the product of intellect and reason. He is now courted and popular, and shares with the great soldiers, statesmen, and explorers the gratitude of nations. Yet modern inventors have by no means always found the path to success and wealth an easy one. If the inventors of the olden time often suffered violence and death, those of a later period

have sometimes been forced to face miscon-
ception and ridicule, poverty and long enduring privations, injustice and robbery, before
they reached the goal of their ambition.
A striking illustration of this fact is found
in the life of Elias Howe, the inventor of the
sewing-machine ; and in that life, also, we are
able to discover qualities as noble and brave,
a perseverance as sturdy and enduring, as
were seen in Palissy, Arkwright, and Watt.
Elias Howe's life, indeed, presents a touching
picture of trials and troubles long continued,
borne with courage and patience, and crowned
at last with a grand success.

It is interesting that many of the foremost
of modern American inventors were born and
brought up, not in the busy cities, but among
the green hills and valleys of the country.
Eli Whitney, W. T. G. Morton (who claimed
to have discovered the use of ether in deaden-
ing pain), and Elias Howe were all sons of
New England farmers.   Howe was a native

of the beautiful town of Spencer, which is spread on the crest of high hills in central Massachusetts. His father was both farmer and miller; and Howe's boyhood's years were spent amid quiet rustic scenes. When Elias was a child, no one would have guessed that he was destined to do any great thing in the world; for he was small of size, feeble in health, and suffered from lameness in one foot from his birth. His father was very poor, and as soon as the little lad was able to work at all, he helped his father in the mill and on the farm.

When he was eleven years old, Elias was "put out," or apprenticed, to a neighboring farmer; but in a short time, being unable to endure the hard farm-work, he returned for a while to his father's mill. Already he began to take an interest in tools and machinery. He mended furniture, and during his spare hours spent his time in learning the use of such tools as his father had, and making

all sorts of things with them. His fondness
for mechanics developed rapidly, and, at six-
teen, resolute of will though frail of body, he
set out from his country home and repaired
to the great manufacturing town of Lowell.
He worked for two years in the Lowell mills
on small wages, at the same time studying
and mastering the details of the machinery
which was used in them.

Then he moved to Waltham, and went to
work in the mills there. At Waltham was
working, at the same time, a cousin of Elias
Howe, who has since become famous both as
a statesman and as a soldier. This was
Nathaniel P. Banks. The two cousins little
thought, when they were toiling at the Waltham looms, that one would become Speaker
of the National House of Representatives,
Governor of Massachusetts, and a major-gener-
al in the army ; and that the other would grow
to be forever famous as one of the greatest
inventors of all time.

While he was in the mills Elias grew more
and more interested in machinery, and he
soon began to dream of being an inventor.
This led him, when he was about twenty
years old, to repair to Boston, where he found
an employer who was an inventor, and who
kept a shop in Cornhill. In this shop Elias
earned nine dollars a week. He now fell in
love, and although he was earning but a small
pittance, he was imprudent enough to get
married. The early days of his wedded life
were full of hardship and privation ; but all
was borne with cheerful courage by him and
his young wife. Unfortunately his health,
never strong, broke down completely, and his
wife and child were brought to the brink of
starvation.

It was while their fortunes were at this low
ebb that the idea struck Elias Howe which
was destined to give him a new object in life,
and which was to lead him, through many
misfortunes and miseries, to fame and for-

tune. His awakening to the knowledge of his powers of invention was as sudden as that of Edmund Cartwright, who invented the power-loom, and as romantic as that of William Lee, the inventor of the stocking-frame. Love, indeed, was the wizard which called his inventive genius into action. Howe sat by his young wife one day in their dismal lodging, not knowing where the next day's food would come from, and with starvation staring them in the face. The wife was busily sewing, and Howe was watching her fingers as they busily plied the needle. All of a sudden the question occurred to him whether a machine could not be made, which, imitating the human fingers, would take stitches many times faster than his wife could do? By a little thought, it seemed to him that such a machine might take fifty stitches while his wife was taking one.

This idea, when once it had got fixed in his mind, never left it. He went to work at once, thinking out the plan of such a machine. He first attempted to attain his object with a needle which had its eye in the middle, and which was sharp at both ends. Then, with difficulty, he made, with pieces of wood and bits of wire, a rude model, which, however rude it was, convinced him that, with toil and patience, a real working sewing-machine could be constructed.

He moved to Cambridge, where his father was living, and he now had the good-fortune to fall in with a friend, George Fisher, who lent him five hundred dollars to continue his experiments, and soon after took Howe and his family into his own house. After the lapse of six months Howe had completed his first machine, which was about a foot and a half high. He showed it to the Boston tailors, but some of them laughed him to scorn, others feared that it would ruin the tailoring trade if it were brought into use; not one of them would purchase it. Then came a period of bitter trials and ill-health, during which Howe depended upon charity for sustenance. But not then, or ever, did misfortune discourage the soul or shake the faith of Elias Howe.

We see him, just as soon as he could raise as much as a pittance, taking passage in the steerage of a sailing-vessel for London, cooking his own food as he made the cheerless voyage across the ocean ; giving the use of his machine to a capitalist in London, who, as soon as his workmen had learned how to manage the sewing-machine, cast Howe adrift ; Howe pawning his clothes to pay for the wretched supply of beans which barely kept body and soul together ; spending four months in making a machine, which he sold for twenty-five dollars ; and, at last, drawing his baggage in a hand-cart to the vessel in which he had engaged himself as a steerage cook, and returning weary, but never despairing, to his native land.

He arrived in New York to learn that his devoted wife was dying at Cambridge; and he had not money enough to make the journey thither. He earned it in a New York machine shop, and reached his wife's bedside just in time to see her die. So poor was he that he was forced to borrow a suit of clothes in which to follow her to her grave. A few days after, he heard that the ship which contained all his worldly goods had gone to the bottom of the sea.

Yet Elias Howe stoutly persevered, and rose bravely above all his difficulties. At last the sewing-machine was introduced, successfully established, and came into rapid demand on every hand. At the age of thirty-five his income from this great invention was two hundred thousand dollars a year. At forty-eight he was worth two millions. His later life, rich and famous though he was, was not one of ease and idle luxury. He dispensed generous and quiet charities; he was kind and benevolent, and especially so toward women in distress; and he was earnestly patriotic.

For this millionnaire, lame as he was, and wearied as he well might have been after such a life of toil and trials, was one of the first to respond to the call to arms at the outbreak of the civil war. He enlisted in the army as a private; shouldered his musket, and went into the ranks; and when, on one occasion, the pay of his regiment (the Seventeenth Connecticut) was behindhand, he himself promptly advanced the thirty thousand dollars needed to supply the wants of his fellow-soldiers. Not long after the close of the war, Elias Howe, not yet an old man, died, leaving the record of a noble, generous, upright life, and a name ever to be honored among the great inventors of the age.

CHAPTER XVIII

IRON AND ITS WORKERS

WITH the advent of iron the whole face of human life was changed. By its aid, it became possible to erect secure dwellings, so that man ceased to be a wanderer and settled down permanently on one spot. By its means, the art of agriculture took its rise. The creation of a home and a farm resulted in settlements, hamlets, villages, thriving towns, and, finally, in the political and social relations which lie at the base of modern civilization.

When, indeed, we consider the wide range of uses to which iron can be put, uses so opposite as "a steel pen and a railroad, the needle of a mariner's compass and a Krupp cannon, a surgeon's lancet and a steam-engine, the delicate mainspring of a watch and an iron-clad man of war, a pair of scissors and a Nasmyth hammer, a lady's ear-ring and a tubular bridge," we can see what a vast change it has wrought in the material condition of the human race.

Of the original discovery that this dull and unlovely metal, hidden in its rough ore, and concealed by its jagged matrix, could be turned to innumerable uses by man, there is no authentic trace, or scarcely a credible tradition. There is, indeed, an ancient story that the qualities of iron were first brought to light by the burning of a forest in Greece; that the charcoal thus formed turned the ore of a mine beneath into the malleable metal. But this story has the character of dim legend rather than of proved history.

The first certain fact about iron is this, that its discovery marked the beginning of the epoch, in man's industrial progress, which has lasted down to the present day. After centuries of dispute, men of science are now agreed in dividing the natural history of human civilization into three ages, according to the material of which the implements used in each age were made.

First, there was the epoch of stone, in which the weapons and utensils were of wood, bone, and yet more frequently of stone and flint. The second age was that of bronze, in which a metal composed of copper and tin took the place of the ruder and simpler materials of old. Bronze, of course, with its greater hardness, and its capacity of being to some degree, at least, sharpened, afforded implements far more effective in the felling of trees, the hewing of stones, the building of boats, and the tilling of land, than those which it replaced. Then came the third epoch, that of the mysterious metal, iron.

No doubt these periods somewhat over-lapped each other. In the bronze age, flint and bones were still somewhat used; for bronze was expensive, and could only be employed sparingly. It was the same in the early part of the iron age. Stone and bronze implements survived for a while, even after iron had not only been found, but smelted and forged into practical use.

With iron, however, the human race started forth upon a new career, and took its first step upwards towards the civilization of to-day.

Iron has never been displaced by any other metal or natural agency. It is still "the soul of manufacture," still the basis upon which the greatest discoveries of modern times are built up.

There is nothing more striking in the history of industry than the eagerness with which men, as soon as they found it, seized on, glorified, and multiplied the capacities of iron. Gold, with all its glitter, beauty, and precious value, sank into the background before this powerful though grimy and uncouth rival. When Crœsus was boasting of his vast golden treasures, the wise Solon retorted on him, —

"If another comes that hath better iron than you, he will be master of all that gold."

When, in the Seven Years' War, an alchemist offered to convert all the Duke of Brunswick's iron into gold, that wise warrior replied, —

"By no means. I want all the iron I can find to resist my enemies. As for gold, I can get it from England."

So late, indeed, as the time of the English Edward the Third, the pots, spits, and frying-pans of the royal kitchen were considered to be among the king's jewels. The nations which used iron weapons against those who did not were the conquering nations; and always, in the wars, the army which fought with the most and best iron weapons overcame their foes. Wherever a people with iron came into collision with a people who had only stone and bronze, the former extirpated and replaced the latter.

One of the most signal instances of the triumphs of iron is seen in the foundation, by its use in war, of the once mighty Turkish Empire. The Turks were originally the wretched, hopeless slaves of a barbarous Oriental ruler. But they lived in an iron district, and they were set at work by their master, forging weapons of iron for his wars. At last, an able and valiant Turk persuaded his fellow-slaves to use the weapons they thus made to secure their own liberties. They poured down from their mountain defiles, assailed the tyrant and his legions, and thus won their freedom. "For centuries after," says an account of this thrilling event, "the Turkish nation continued to celebrate their liberation by an annual ceremony, in which a piece of iron was heated in the fire, and a smith's hammer was successively handled by the prince and his nobles."

The Philistines knew well the advantage held by a people who forged and used weapons of iron. We read in the Bible that, in completing their conquest of the Israelites, they captured and carried off all the smiths in Judea; "for the Philistines said, Lest the Hebrews make them swords or spears. But the Israelites went down to the Philistines to sharpen every man his share, his coulter, and his axe, and his mattocks."

When the tribes and nations found out the uses of iron, they valued it so preciously that, in their ignorance and superstition, they were tempted to worship it as something sacred and divine. The Romans called it " Mars," after their god of war; and Captain Cook tells us that the New Zealanders of the last century were ready to pay homage to the axe, as to a deity, to offer sacrifices to the saw, and to make an idol of the knife. The inventor of the saw, indeed, was exalted by the Greeks to a seat among their gods.

It naturally followed from this veneration for iron, a homage awarded to it alone among metals, that a lofty place should be given by common consent to the workers in iron. In remote ages, therefore, and indeed, in ages not very remote, the smith was truly a hero among his fellows. The ancient smith was honored on all occasions with special honors and privileges. He was a man of rare and various accomplishments.

"He made nails," says a recent writer, "and shod horses; he fashioned axes, saws, adzes, chisels, augers, and hammers for the mechanics, and spades and hoes for the farmers; he devised bolts and chains for the castle-gates of the great barons, and fastenings for their bridges and portcullises. But especially was the smith valued as the artificer of the weapons and appliances of war and of barbaric sports. He made and mended the weapons used in the chase and in war, the gavelocks, bills, and battle-axes;

he tipped the bowmen's arrows, and furnished spear-heads for the men-at-arms. But, above all, he forged the mail-coats and cuirasses of the chiefs, and welded those huge swords on the temper and quality of which life, honor, and victory depended on the battle-field."

In the Anglo-Saxon period of English history, the smith was indeed a mighty man. He sat at royal tables, below the court chaplain, and above the court physician. At the court of Wales it was provided that the smith was entitled to a draught of every kind of liquor that was brought into the king's dining-hall. Special laws guarded the safety of his person. Once a Scottish smith committed a crime for which the penalty was death. But so precious were his services to the chief of his clan, that the latter ordered that two weavers should be hanged in his stead.

The common people often attributed to the smith supernatural power. He who could forge swords like the sword "Excalibur" of

King Arthur and the sword "Joyeuse" of Charlemagne, weapons which were themselves regarded as inanimate heroes, and had names as if they were living warriors, must, thought the Saxon churl, be endowed with magical powers. The names of the great smiths of the Saxon and mediæval times are as familiar in legend and chronicle as are those of the kings and the Crusaders. Weland, the smith, is closely bound up with the heroic traditions of King Arthur. The dark smith of Drontheim is the hero of Norwegian tales. Henry Ferrers, the smith who went in William the Conqueror's train, is almost as renowned as the Conqueror himself ; and his descendant, the present Earl Ferrers, bears the sign of his origin from the anvil, in the six horse-shoes which appear on his coat-of-arms.

There are few more brilliant names in the annals of industrial art than that of Andrea de Ferrera, who forged, in the Highlands of

Scotland, swords which rivalled in their fine temper and ductile strength, the famous blades of Damascus, Milan, and Toledo.

In the middle ages in England, the smith had become by all odds the most important and skilful personage in the working community. His achievements were now no longer confined to the making of implements, weapons, and armor. He seemed indeed to be "the rivet which held society together." He was the farrier and veterinary surgeon, the dentist and sometimes the doctor, the parish clerk and the news-monger of his district. The smithy was the universal resort where to receive and discuss the tidings of the day; and of all those who discussed the news the smith was by far the most learned and the most respectfully listened to. The smithy was thus "the very eye and tongue of the village."

In early times, the surnames of men were often derived from their callings; and, as the

smith was the earliest and most highly considered of all men who worked with their
hands, so the name of Smith became, and
has continued to this day, the most frequently met with of all English surnames.
Not only is this true of English names; in
other tongues, we find that the equivalent of
" Smith " is more common than other names.
" Schmidt " in German, " Cowan " in Scottish,
" Fabri " in Italian, " Lefevre " in French,
mean precisely what Smith means in English.
Our modern " Mr. Smith," therefore, need
not blush for his name, nor be nettled by the
witticisms and amusement with which it is
sometimes greeted. For his surname is high
and ancient. He can boast of an ancestry
revered and honored when the ancestors of
England's haughtiest nobles and America's
proudest families, nay, when the ancestors of
some crowned monarchs, were savages roam-
ing the forests, or robbers desolating domains
and burning villages !

It has only been within the past two hundred years that the progress of iron manufacture has been rapid, and that its uses have become well-nigh universal. This is owing to the fact that it was not until the seventeenth century that Dud Dudley discovered the art of smelting iron with pit-coal. In all the preceding centuries iron had been slowly smelted with charcoal. It was Dudley's invention which began the revolution in iron manufacture, by which it has truly become, as John Locke called it, "the author of plenty," in our own age.

HISTORICAL BOOKS • • • •
• • • • FOR YOUNG PEOPLE

Young Folks' History of the United States

By THOMAS WENTWORTH HIGGINSON. Illustrated. $1.50.

The story of our country in the most reliable and interesting form. As a story-book it easily leads all other American history stories in interest, while as a text-book for the study of history it is universally admitted to be the best.

Young Folks' Book of American Explorers

By THOMAS WENTWORTH HIGGINSON. Uniform with the "Young Folks' History of the United States." One volume, fully illustrated. Price $1.50.

" It is not a history told in the third person, nor an historical novel for young folks, where the author supposes the chief characters to have thought and said such and such things under such and such circumstances; but it is the genuine description given by the persons who experienced the things they described in letters written home." — *Montpelier Journal.*

The Nation in a Nutshell

By GEORGE MAKEPEACE TOWLE, author of " Heroes of History," " Young Folks' History of England," " Young Folks' History of Ireland," etc. Price 50 cents.

" To tell the story of a nation like ours in a nutshell, requires a peculiar faculty for selecting, condensing, and philosophizing. The brevity with which he relates the principal events in American history, does not detract from the charming interest of the narrative style." — *Public Opinion.*

Young People's History of England

By GEORGE MAKEPEACE TOWLE. Cloth, illustrated. $1.50.

" The whole narrative is made interesting and attractive — in every way what a book of this kind should be in its clearness of statement, freshness of style, and its telling of the right ways." — *Critic.*

Handbook of English History

Based on " Lectures on English History," by the late M. J. GUEST, and brought down to the year 1880. With a Supplementary Chapter on the English Literature of the 19th Century. By F. H. UNDERWOOD, LL.D. With Maps, Chronological Table, etc. $1.50.

" It approaches nearer perfection than anything in the line we have seen. It is succinct, accurate, and delightful." — *Hartford Evening Post.*

Young People's History of Ireland

By GEORGE MAKEPEACE TOWLE, author of " Young People's History of England," " Young Folks' Heroes of History," etc. With an introduction by JOHN BOYLE O'REILLY. Cloth, illustrated. $1.50.

" The history is like a novel, increasing in interest to the very end, and terminating at the most interesting period of the whole; and the reader lays down the book a moment in enthusiastic admiration for a people who have endured so much, and yet have retained so many admirable characteristics." — *N. Y. World.*

Sold by all booksellers, and sent by mail, postpaid, on receipt of price

LEE AND SHEPARD Publishers Boston